"I feel really bad, making such work for you."

"It's nothing."

"But—"

Tate gave a firm shake of his head. "Tomorrow afternoon I'll be over here to help with the cleanup. Okay?"

"No. You have a lot to do as it is. I'll take care of it."

"Neighbors help each other around here, Sara. And believe me, if you don't let me pitch in, I will never hear the end of it from my grandma."

Sara stared at the blackened garage for a long moment, her eyes weary and a little dazed.

"You're a good man, Tate. I'd forgotten just how kind you are."

Then she hurried to her truck without a backward glance.

He stared after her, the world shifting beneath his feet.

Since she'd come back to town, nothing had been said. No parameters had been discussed. But he'd understood their tacit agreement— whatever they'd had between them was in the past, and _____ rs now.

So why _____ o mean so much

A *USA TODAY* bestselling and award-winning author of over thirty-five novels, **Roxanne Rustand** lives in the country with her husband and a menagerie of pets, including three horses, rescue dogs and cats. She has a master's in nutrition and is a clinical dietitian. *RT Book Reviews* nominated her for a Career Achievement Award, two of her books won their annual Reviewers' Choice Award and two others were nominees.

Books by Roxanne Rustand

Love Inspired

Rocky Mountain Ranch

Montana Mistletoe
High Country Homecoming
Snowbound with the Cowboy

Aspen Creek Crossroads

Winter Reunion
Second Chance Dad
The Single Dad's Redemption
An Aspen Creek Christmas
Falling for the Rancher

Love Inspired Suspense

Big Sky Secrets

Fatal Burn
End Game
Murder at Granite Falls
Duty to Protect

Visit the Author Profile page at Harlequin.com for more titles.

Snowbound with the Cowboy

Roxanne Rustand

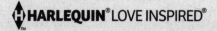

LOVE INSPIRED BOOKS

Recycling programs
for this product may
not exist in your area.

ISBN-13: 978-1-335-48791-9

Snowbound with the Cowboy

www.Harlequin.com

Printed in U.S.A.

And all things, whatsoever ye shall ask
in prayer, believing, ye shall receive.
—*Matthew* 21:22

With love to Larry, Andy, Brian and Emily.
And with love always and forever
to my dear mother, Arline, who supported me
every step of the way on my writing journey.

Chapter One

"Got it. A two-year-old gelding, lacerations to the pastern and fetlock." Sara Branson stared down at the clipboard braced against the steering wheel of her vet truck and tried to rein in her roiling emotions. "But tell me again. This is *where*?"

"It's part of the Langford Ranch—but go three miles past the main gate, then turn west." The male voice seemed vaguely familiar. "This section of the ranch used to be the old Branson place. The house and barns are—"

"Two miles from the highway, at the end of a long, curving lane." Where a backdrop of pine-blanketed foothills climbed up to the base of the Montana Rockies, and the sun dropped behind those rugged, snow-covered peaks every night.

She knew the property very well.

But to her, it *wasn't* part of the Langford Ranch and never would be. It had been her aunt and uncle's ranch until eight years ago, when the bank abruptly foreclosed and Gus Langford snapped it up under shady circumstances.

"Uh…right." The male voice hesitated. "So you've been out here before and know where to go?"

That was the understatement of the year, and the whole sad situation still made her heart ache. "I'm just leaving a ranch north of Pine Bend. I'll be there in—" she consulted the GPS on the dashboard of her truck "—roughly thirty-five minutes. Are you the foreman?"

"In a matter of speaking." His short laugh wasn't very convincing. "Temporarily, anyhow."

He ended the call before she could ask his name.

By the time she arrived and pulled to a stop in front of the horse barn, she'd lectured herself back into the calm, professional persona of the good veterinarian she was.

This was simply another vet call. No personal issues. No anger over the past. Nothing could change what had happened, after all. And the man who'd called her was just some employee who'd had nothing to do with Gus Langford's actions, so he certainly didn't deserve any snarky comments from her.

But she still wished she could give the late Gus Langford a piece of her mind.

She surveyed the two-story log house at the far side of the parking area in front of the barns, where she'd stayed for long stretches during the school year, whenever her parents had temporarily split up over one ruckus or another, plus every summer until she graduated from high school. Aunt Millie and Uncle Warren had been like a second set of parents in a stable, warm and loving home.

But even from here she could see the wraparound porch was sagging and the roof needed repair, and as she pivoted to look at the barns, they seemed to be in even worse shape.

Langford, rest his soul, had been one of the richest ranchers in the county. If he'd been so determined to steal this place from her aunt and uncle, why hadn't he bothered with maintenance afterward?

He'd probably cared only about gaining the additional grazing land for his vast herds of cattle. And *nothing* about the love and dreams and backbreaking work that had gone into making this place a home, which made the situation seem even worse. She'd been a classmate to Tate Langford, one of Gus's sons, and had seen his two older brothers around town while growing up. They'd all been decent kids, far as she knew, but over the years they'd probably grown up to be just like their father.

Grabbing her satchel from the seat next to her, she rounded the back of her truck and swiftly added extra supplies from the various doors in the vet box. Sutures. Surgical equipment. IV sedative. Antibiotics. Sterile saline for flushing the wounds. Bandaging materials.

No one had come out of the house, the machine shed or the two barns to greet her when she arrived, so she headed straight for the horse barn. The tractor-wide double doors were closed against the mid-February bite in the air, so she opened the smaller walk door and stepped inside to the sound of an old country song blaring on the radio.

A wave of nostalgia washed over her as she took in the long cement aisle flanked with a dozen box stalls on each side. Pine paneling rose halfway up each stall front and its sliding door, with vertical metal pipes forming the barrier along the top half of the stalls for ventilation and visibility.

Partway down, a young sorrel stood cross-tied in the middle of the aisle with a broad-shouldered man in jeans and black shirt hunkered down at its side. He was expertly wrapping one of its front legs.

"Hello, there," she called out. "I'm Dr. Branson. Someone called, and—"

The man finished the last wrap of the bandage around the leg, stood abruptly and turned to face her, his expression stunned. *"Sara?"*

"Tate?" Her heart flip-flopped in her chest. She felt as stunned as he looked, and it took a moment to find her voice with so many painful high school memories crashing through her thoughts.

Guilt.

Remorse.

Heartache.

In high school, the first time he'd angled a heart-stopping grin in her direction she'd felt herself falling, falling into the depths of his silver-blue gaze, too mesmerized to even speak, even though she'd known he was way too wild and irresponsible—a magnet for the popular, flirty girls. Not a guy who'd want a plain, ordinary nerd like her.

But nothing had ever been predictable where Tate Langford was concerned.

"W-what are you doing here?"

He blinked. "That was *you* on the phone?"

"Calls roll over to my cell phone if the clinic receptionist is on another line." She tipped her head slightly. "Guess I forgot to introduce myself."

"As did I." He shook his head in disbelief. "It's been a long time."

"Fourteen years." She felt a flare of warmth in her cheeks, realizing it sounded as if she had been actually paying close attention to that passage of time all these years, like some lovesick puppy. "I mean—since high school graduation."

"And now you're the vet in town." He lifted an eyebrow. "Quite an improvement over the crotchety old buzzard who owned the clinic years ago. Knowing what he was like, I'm sure he drove a hard bargain."

"I don't know. The vet who bought the practice from

him left to join her fiancé's practice in Idaho. I signed the papers a few weeks ago."

"I thought your parents wanted you to go to med school, like they did."

"Adamantly. But I had a change of heart." Coupled with a surge of rebellion leading to an estrangement that still hadn't fully healed.

Life hadn't been any easier for Tate, though, given his father's reputation as a controlling, volatile man who never backed down. In high school, Tate had once told her that he hated the ranch and couldn't wait to leave. And once he did, he was never, ever coming back.

She cocked her head and studied him. "I remember *your* dad wanted every one of his sons to stay on the ranch. But by the time I left for college I heard all of you had left. For good."

"Yeah, my dad's plans didn't work out so well, either. All of us dreamed of escaping the ranch, and we did." A corner of Tate's mouth lifted in a wry smile. "Devlin went into the Marines, Jess left to rodeo and then I followed suit. When we disrupted Dad's plans for building his ranching dynasty, he was so riled that he told us to never come back. He was not a forgiving man."

She furrowed her brow, thinking. "I've only been back a few weeks, but I think I might have seen Jess around town."

"Probably. When Dad got Parkinson's he wasn't happy about swallowing his pride and asking Jess to come back. Ironic, because Jess had been saving his rodeo earnings for vet school, and gave up his own dreams to take over the ranch. Dad died a year later, and I doubt he ever thanked Jess for coming home."

"What about Devlin?"

"He was severely injured in a bomb blast, and got a

medical discharge from the Marines. He moved back last spring. Now he's an active partner in the ranch."

"So you and your brothers ended up ranching after all."

Tate rested a hand on the gelding's sleek neck. "Not me. I came back a few days ago, and I'll be home for just a few months. Too many bad memories here to suit me."

"I don't blame you."

In grade school, he'd lost a younger sister in a tragic accident, and less than a year later his mother died. The whole town knew how harsh Gus had been with his sons after that. For all of their land and wealth, no one would've wanted to be in their shoes.

Which made her own behavior toward Tate in high school seem all the worse. Maybe he didn't remember anything about it, after all these years, but seeing him again made that emotional baggage weigh heavily on her heart.

She swallowed hard and shook off her thoughts as she approached the two-year-old gelding, ran a comforting hand down his neck and shoulder and carefully unwrapped the leg. "You've done a good job of keeping this leg clean. He's up to date on all of his vaccinations, right? Including tetanus?"

Tate nodded. "I checked his records. All good."

"What happened?"

"Barbwire," he said with disgust. "If I was going to stay here longer, I'd have time to replace all of it with something safer—at least around the horse pastures. Some cattle went through the fence last night. At least a hundred head of Angus were in the horse pasture this morning, and by then, this colt had gotten tangled up in the downed wire."

"The cattle probably didn't even see the fence during that heavy snowfall. Did you get them all rounded up?"

"Yep. At least they were contained in an adjoining pasture. My brothers came over to help drive them back."

She administered an intravenous sedative, and waited until the gelding's head sleepily lowered. After injecting some anesthetic, she examined the edges of the lacerations, flushed them with sterile saline and probed the depths of the wounds.

She retrieved suture materials from her satchel and got to work. "I'm only suturing the cannon bone area," she said without looking away from the leg. "Fortunately, the wounds on the pastern are minor. In that area, sutures tend to pull out when the joint flexes. I'd have to do something more involved."

When she finished, she wrapped the leg in gauze, then fluffy white sheet cotton, followed by stretchy Vetrap to thoroughly stabilize the dressing.

After she'd administered an injection of IM antibiotics, she stowed her gear back into the satchel and pulled off her vinyl gloves. "Stall rest only. I need to see this horse in three or four days, and then a week or two after that. Will someone be around, say, on Thursday morning around eleven?"

"Sure. Just give me a call if anything changes." He slowly led the injured gelding into a stall and unbuckled his halter, then stepped out and slid the door shut.

A wave of memories washed over her as she breathed in the familiar scents of sawdust bedding and good mixed alfalfa and grass hay. "I was…surprised to be called out here. Has anyone lived here since my aunt and uncle lost the place?" She'd tried to still the edge in her voice but apparently hadn't succeeded, because she saw a flash of sympathy in Tate's eyes.

"I'd left for college and then the rodeo circuit before that, but by the looks of the house, I don't think anyone has lived here in years. So what happened to your aunt and uncle?"

"Years of drought, low livestock prices. Mounting medical bills for Millie's cancer. They took out loans against the ranch to try to hang on, but they ended up sinking in debt they couldn't repay." She dredged up a weak smile. "Yet they still kept sending me a little money every month to help with my rent. I was away at college and they never said a word about how bad things were. They didn't want me to worry. When I learned the truth it just about broke my heart."

"Sounds like there was no hope of recovering."

"Warren was sure they could've rallied if only they'd had just a few more months. But the bank abruptly called in their loans and wouldn't even *talk* about an extension. And your dad—" She bit back the sharp words on her lips.

She would never believe there hadn't been something fishy going on between the bank president and Gus Langford to precipitate that sudden foreclosure and sale. But there was no going back. Gus was dead and the whole situation was past history.

And none of it was Tate's fault.

"Some folks said Dad was like a vulture. He never missed a chance to grab what he wanted." A faint, sad smile touched a corner of Tate's mouth. "Where are your aunt and uncle now?"

"After the foreclosure they had just enough equity to pay off their legal fees, settle their debts, and scrape together the money for a small, remote cabin. They live in town now, though."

She gave Tate a cool nod of farewell, but he followed her out to her truck anyway and opened the door for her, then stepped back as she lifted the satchel onto the front seat and climbed behind the steering wheel.

He closed the door for her. "Thanks, Sara. I appreciate you coming by so quickly."

"No problem." She glanced over at him through the open window and their eyes locked for a moment too long before she jerked her gaze away and started the engine.

He'd changed a lot since she'd last seen him at high school graduation. He was much taller, his shoulders had broadened. His voice was deeper.

He still had those trademark Langford eyes, though. The dark, sweeping eyebrows and stunning silver-blue eyes with long dark lashes. With that black hair and an easy, lopsided grin that deepened the slash of a dimple in his left cheek, he could probably charm any woman with a pulse from nine to ninety.

Every one of the brothers was perfect material for the cover of *GQ* magazine, though their saving grace was that none of them had ever seemed to realize it.

She'd fallen under his spell in high school, but that was long over. Even if she felt the *smallest* twinge of attraction now, the Langfords had destroyed the two people who loved her most. And after that, empty charm and stunning good looks didn't matter—not to her. There'd be no point at any rate. Tate intended to leave town.

But Pine Bend was now her permanent home, and she never would.

Jess tossed another bale of hay off of the hayrack hitched to his truck and grinned down at Tate. "So the new vet in town is your old girlfriend, right? Did she ask you out on a date?"

Tate hefted the bale and carried it into the horse barn. "Not my old girlfriend," he called over his shoulder. "It was a class of thirty. We all knew each other."

"Not how I remember it." Jess threw off another bale.

"Seems to me you two dated for a while, your senior year. I remember, because I'd already left for college but I was a tad jealous when I heard about it. A pretty girl like that— a guy like you—it sure didn't make sense to me. And she was a doctor's daughter, to boot. High-class. How did you manage it, anyway?"

Ignoring him, Tate hauled the bale into the barn and tossed it up to Devlin, who was standing on top of the stack in the rapidly filling hay stall just inside the door.

Devlin leveled a cocky look down at him. "I'm real curious too. Of course, back then you hadn't gone off to rodeo just yet. You didn't hobble around like Methuselah."

"Like you?" Tate retorted, then immediately wished he could call his teasing words back.

Devlin had been through countless surgeries and rounds of physical therapy before receiving a medical discharge from the Marines. Even if they were all just taunting each other right now, Dev deserved only respect for all he'd been through.

But Dev just grinned back at him. "So, she's coming back this morning to check on that injured gelding. Right? Will we get to see romantic sparks fly? Hey, Jess, look— Tate's *blushing*."

"Am not," Tate shot back. "With luck, you'll both be gone by then. You're gonna embarrass that poor woman to death."

"Us?" Jess tossed two more bales off the truck and melodramatically flapped a hand against his chest. "We don't want to kid around with her—we want to make sure she has good intentions toward our baby brother."

"Yep," Dev concurred gravely. "You're still not married at thirty-two, so you obviously need our help."

Tate snickered. "Maybe you two needed mine. Jess didn't get married till last June, and you didn't even get

engaged till that same weekend. You two weren't exactly speedy, either."

Twenty more bales flew off the hayrack in rapid succession, a brief pause, then the final ten. Jess climbed off the empty rack and helped Tate toss the rest of the bales up to Devlin.

When the job was done, Tate stood back, took off his leather gloves and slapped them against his thigh to knock off the hay dust. The hay stall was full. Up in the hayloft, there wasn't room for another bale, and outside, rows of big round bales of hay were stored for the cows.

"Thanks, guys. I'd forgotten about what a good feeling it is to have a barn full of hay."

"Now we just need to get you to *stay* for good," Jess said dryly. "What are the chances of you changing your mind?"

"Still pretty much zero." He'd once been a top money earner, but ten years of rodeo injuries had taken a relentless physical toll and his days of competing were over. "I still plan to buy that rodeo stock contractor's company at his dispersal sale on May 2nd. Livestock, equipment and all. It has one of the best reputations in the country, so I could step in and get right back to following the rodeo circuit. I miss that life."

Devlin lifted an eyebrow. "You were a competitor, sure. But what do you know about producing rodeos?"

"I'm not interested in producing the whole event. Just contracting to supply all of the livestock they need, then hauling it to the various rodeo grounds."

"If you care for cattle that much, you have plenty of livestock right here."

Tate snorted. "Beef cattle and bucking bulls aren't the same."

"On what planet? They all moo." The corner of Devlin's mouth quirked up in a grin at his own lame joke. "And here you've got a fine house to live in, on a spread with a stellar view of the Rockies…an old girlfriend coming to call…"

"Have you *looked* in that house? It's been an adventure, from the first day I moved in."

"No, but…"

"Jess?"

"Uh…no. Not since I came back to Montana to help dad out. A couple years, now. With a broom and a little dusting…"

"Oh, I cleaned it up the best I could when I moved in. But please, let me give you a tour." Tate led them across the wide parking area to the tumbledown picket fence surrounding the yard, then to the rickety wooden steps leading up to the sagging wraparound covered porch. "Watch your step. Some of these boards are—"

One of the porch floorboards splintered under Devlin's boot and he nimbly stepped to one side. "Challenging?"

"Dangerous." Tate opened the back screen door and ushered them into the large country kitchen, with its yellowed linoleum flooring curling at the edges and Harvest Gold appliances dating back to the 1970s. "The fridge runs at around fifty degrees and two of the stove burners don't work. The furnace is so old that I try to avoid starting it, so thank goodness the fireplace checked out all right."

"Nice and cozy, then."

"Sheer practicality. I had to turn the water back on when I moved in, so when the outside temp drops into the thirties I have to light a fire to keep the pipes from freezing."

Jess looked at the faded, peeling wallpaper and cleared his throat. "A month or two of work and—"

"No, really. Just keep going." Tate waved them on toward the living room, where an open staircase led up to the bedrooms. "You haven't experienced this place until you've seen the water damage on the ceilings upstairs. Some are actually bowing downward. Oh, and the breeze whistles right through those window frames. It's mighty chilly."

Upstairs, the brothers roamed through the three bedrooms and the solitary bathroom, where the squeaky floor hinted at rotting floorboards beneath a shabby avocado shag carpet. The house was a disaster—Tate couldn't deny it. Yet, as he glanced around, he imagined Sara living here with her loving aunt and uncle. Conversation around the dinner table. Christmas celebrations. The kind of warm family life he'd longed for after his mother died. How could he let it all go to ruin?

"I get the drift," Devlin muttered. "The place is a wreck. Apparently Dad didn't figure the place was worth saving."

"But it is," Tate countered. "The house has good bones. It just needs work. Though if the problems aren't dealt with soon, it will be nothing but a pile of firewood."

"Exactly." Devlin prodded at the musty carpeting with the toe of his boot. "I vote for demolition."

Jess studied the stained ceiling above the top of the stairs. "Tate?"

"Hiring a remodeling company would cost a fortune. You probably couldn't even find one willing to come out this far." Tate rested a hand on the wobbly staircase banister and gave it a light shake. "The rodeo contractor's dispersal sale is the beginning of May, so I won't be here long enough to get everything done. But, Jess, you gave up the career you wanted, to take over the ranch. And, Dev, you came back too. I owe you guys, and I want to do all I can to help. I haven't been around to do my share."

Jess started down the stairs. "So what do you propose?"

"I can pull together some numbers on what has to be done, the materials and how much it will cost. If you two agree, I'll tackle as much as I can while I'm here. For some of the labor I might need extra hands, if one of you can spare the time."

"Both of us can, but Dev is handier than I am. Since coming home, he renovated two of the three cabins over at the home place." A sly grin lifted a corner of Jess's mouth. "And who knows? Dev thought he was just gonna stay awhile, then move on. Now he's running the adjoining Cavanaugh spread that Dad bought years ago. You might end up staying too. Maybe even here on the Branson place."

Tate laughed at the suggestion, though it brought the past slamming into his thoughts. The last place he'd ever want to live was on a part of the Langford Ranch, where bad memories were lurking at every corner, and his old guilt and anger could resurface without warning.

How did Jess and Devlin cope? Had they somehow buried the past too deeply to even notice anymore?

That seemed impossible.

"Say you do manage to buy that company and its bucking stock." Jess pursed his lips as he surveyed the living room before moving on to the kitchen. "You'll still need time to develop your business plan, advertise and start to schedule rodeo dates for next year. Maybe you'll need to stay here longer than you think—at least until you get on your feet."

"What about the livestock semitrailers you'll need for going cross-country to rodeos?" Devlin interjected.

Tate snorted. "I appreciate all of the fatherly advice, but I have it covered. The guy holding the dispersal sale is selling his trailers, and he's willing to work with the winning bidder as a salaried manager for the first year to ensure an easy transition."

Jess rocked back on his heels. "You do know this won't be cheap."

"I found a good broker early on, and invested my rodeo winnings for years. I'll also qualify for business loans." Tate shrugged. "I've always known I couldn't compete forever, so this has been my plan for a long time."

Jess tipped his head toward a window facing the barns. "At least you'll have this—a place to keep the livestock."

"Actually, I'll be looking for something more central—close to Denver, probably."

From outside came the sound of tires crunching across the gravel parking area, then pulling to a stop.

Devlin skated a sidelong look at Tate and raised an eyebrow. "I guess we're in luck. Now that we've sorted out your new career, we can all go out to greet the vet and see if you have any chance with her at all."

"Maybe we can even help," Jess added with a laugh. "You'll probably need it."

Tate stifled a groan as his childhood memories flooded back.

Jess and Dev had always been bigger, stronger and fiercely competitive with each other. He'd idolized them. Shadowed them. In turn, they'd relentlessly teased him as only older brothers could, and they'd become experts at it.

He didn't need that now.

Even if seeing Sara again had reawakened a glimmer of feelings he'd buried long ago, he had no intention of pursuing her. There was no point, given her career in town and his plans to hit the road.

But both Jess and Dev could make the next few months more than awkward if they decided to make overblown declarations about unrequited love…and embarrassed Sara or gave her the wrong impression.

Hopefully they'd matured beyond the teenage taunts and teasing that all three of them had shared, but he wouldn't put it past them, either.

Still, he had to give them credit.

They'd each found an amazing woman to settle down with, and from what he could see, they'd both found hope and inspiration in their faith. He couldn't lay claim to any of that. The years had made him more cynical.

God hadn't listened to him years ago, when Heather and Mom died, or after his rodeo buddy Jace was injured in a horrific rodeo accident. A good, kind man and a devout Christian, Jace died anyway, leaving a distraught wife and two little kids. Where was God then?

After that it hadn't seemed worth the effort, no matter what Grandma Betty said about God always answering prayers. It had been a while since he'd stepped inside a church. But maybe God would be willing to handle something small.

Listening to his brothers' laughter as they sauntered toward the barn, he glanced heavenward, then briefly closed his eyes and prayed.

Chapter Two

Sara reached across the front seat of her truck to stroke the dog's head, then rested her hand on its thin shoulders. "We're going to find you a good home, Lucy," she murmured. "Someone who will take care of those pups of yours too. I promise."

It wasn't going to be easy. Mostly black, with a white shawl over its neck and shoulders and four tall white socks mottled with black freckles, she looked like an indeterminate mixture of border collie, golden retriever and perhaps a pointer, and the father of her pups was anybody's guess. The folks five miles down the road hadn't known, and hadn't cared. They'd just wanted her *gone*.

She was halfway out of her truck when she spied the three Langford boys—*men*—striding across the parking area toward her.

Even from a distance, she knew they couldn't be anyone else, each of them tall and broad-shouldered, with the same sort of self-confident saunter. No one could mistake them for anything but brothers, though Tate was a bit taller and Jess was a little heavier.

But despite the rocky end to their high school romance years ago, Tate was still the only guy who had ever made her stomach tie itself in knots and made her foolish heart beat a little faster.

She stifled a sigh, wishing this vet call was already over.

Jess reached her first and thrust out his hand. "Good to see you again, Sara. You and Tate were three years behind me, but I remember you from school."

She shook his hand and nodded, then looked over at Devlin and offered her hand to him, forcing herself to avoid any reaction to the scarring that trailed down the side of his temple and disappeared inside his shirt collar. "Devlin. Good to see you again."

"Same here." He shot a quick, indecipherable grin at Tate as he shook her hand. "I hear you recently moved back to Pine Bend. I expect we'll be seeing you out at the ranch quite a bit in the future. For vet calls, that is."

There was an undercurrent of tension—maybe even sly humor—radiating between the three brothers that she couldn't quite read, and she faltered for a split second, then regained her composure. Whatever nonsense was going on between them, she needed to check the injured horse and be on her way. Leaving the Langford place would make the rest of the day seem a whole lot brighter.

"So how is that gelding doing?" she asked briskly as she grabbed her satchel from the backseat of her truck and started for the barn. "Still on stall rest, right?"

"Absolutely." Tate followed her toward the barn.

The other two brothers veered off toward a gleaming black Ford F350 hitched to an empty hay wagon. "See you later," Jess called out. "I've got to meet a cattle buyer this afternoon."

"Thank goodness," Tate muttered under his breath as the truck took off down the lane, light snow boiling up from beneath its tires.

"What?"

He hesitated, then gave her a wry glance. "Dev seems to think you and I were quite an item in high school, and that it never stopped."

She stumbled, but caught herself. "Oh."

"And since he has the tact of a Brahman bull, you might as well be forewarned. I am not responsible for anything he says, implies or does."

She couldn't help but laugh at Tate's pained expression. "I'm not sure I can visualize an ex-Marine as a match-maker."

"Frankly, I think he *and* Jess were just trying to get me riled, but I can only hope for the best."

At the sound of a pitiful bark from her truck she glanced over her shoulder, then continued toward the barn.

But when the dog howled with fear, that stopped her in her tracks. "I'm sorry. That's Lucy. Do you have any dogs loose around here?"

"Nope."

"Do you mind if I let her out of my truck?"

"Go right ahead. She sounds pretty desperate."

Sara went back and lifted the dog down from the seat. Once on the ground, she shivered against Sara's leg.

"Looks like your dog is gonna be a momma, and soon."

"Within a few days, I suspect."

He gave the dog a closer look, then raised his gaze to Sara's and lifted an eyebrow. "Except for that belly, she looks awfully thin."

"I saw her cowering in a snow-filled ditch a few miles down the road. I stopped at the house to ask about her, and the guy said he 'wanted to get rid of her,' because she's pregnant." Sara said a quick, silent prayer of thanks, grateful that she hadn't driven past without noticing. "Pathetic as this is, she spent her life on a heavy log chain with a ramshackle doghouse, but he'd let her loose, quit feeding her and tried to chase her off so she'd move on. Can you imagine? Some people shouldn't be responsible for any living thing."

"I'll agree with you there. At the least, he should have spayed her."

"From the looks of the house I don't think he could afford it, and this county doesn't have a free spay clinic, either." Another one of her goals, she reflected. "At least not yet."

"Are there any animal shelters?"

"Not in this county. The closest is a two-hour drive."

"Some people cast off a dog like trash. But for that dog, home is their whole world—the one family they'll love for their short lifetime, if they're lucky. Heartless people like her owner make me sick."

Tate was watching her intently now, his eyes fixed on hers. She took a slow, deep breath to calm down the anger in her voice. "Sorry, I get a little intense when it comes to animal welfare."

"I wouldn't expect anything less. It's your job."

"*And* my passion." She leaned down to ruffle the fur at the dog's neck. "I'm just so sorry that I can't keep her myself."

"Why not?"

"I'm living in a small cabin, and don't have enough space, or enough time at home to care for her. And the… um…current population there wouldn't exactly be good company for a new mom and her litter of puppies."

"Population?"

She felt her cheeks warm. Most people might think she was crazy, but she hadn't been able to say no to a number of abandoned animals since returning to Pine Bend.

If she gave in one more time she might end up sleeping in her truck. "I just wish I had a bigger place."

The dog waddled into the barn behind her and Tate followed, closing the door after them. He strode to a stall halfway down the aisle and brought out the injured colt.

The gelding tossed his head and did a little sideways jog as if wanting to take off running. "He's pretty impatient to be outside, as you can see."

After Tate cross-tied him, Sara knelt at his side and removed the layers of leg wrap and cotton batting.

"The wounds look good," she said, inspecting them closely. "With just the expected minimal seepage of serous—that's clear—fluid but no evidence of swelling or infection."

After pulling clean materials from her satchel she rebandaged the leg, then gave the gelding another injection of long-acting antibiotics.

"He shouldn't be out in the pasture until the bandages are off and he's fully healed. I'd rather he wasn't free to run and buck just yet. But he could go on a hot-walker if you've got one, or you could pony him around the arena while riding another horse."

"That's what I figured." Tate led the colt back to his stall, took off the halter and came back out to the aisle. "No rush, that's for sure. This is one of the Langford horses that we'll—er, Jess—will put in our production sale next year. Well-broke ranch horses are worth quite a lot these days."

"That's what I like to hear." Sara picked up her satchel. "Is there anything else while I'm here?"

He looked up at a calico barn cat glaring down at them from the rafters. "Jess says the barn cats need rabies vaccinations and whatever other vaccines they ought to have. But I don't expect I can catch them all in a hurry, either."

As if the cat knew she was in danger, she disappeared.

"Are you feeding them cat food or are they just mousers?"

"Both, now. They looked sleek and fat when I got here, but I give them some dry cat food in the tack room anyway, in case they have a bad mouse day. There's three of them, and they come running at *kittykittykitty* in the morning."

She gave him an assessing look. He might be from a wealthy ranching family: the son of the infamously cold and calculating Gus Langford. But from what the younger vet tech in the clinic said, with a good dose of hero worship in her eyes, he'd had a stellar rodeo career with many a championship.

And he still had a soft heart.

"Good. I want to see the colt one last time, in two weeks. Withhold the cat food the day before so they'll be even more eager, then close them in the tack room for me and we can take care of them then."

She whistled to the dog and patted her thigh, signaling for the animal to follow her out to her truck. But the stray looked between her and Tate, then slunk over to him, draped herself over the toes of his boots and looked up at him with pure longing.

"Wait." He looked down into Lucy's pleading eyes and felt his heart melt. "About this dog. What's going to happen to her? She won't be put down, will she?"

Sara drew in a sharp breath, shocked at his words. "Of *course* not. I'll…I'll need to keep her at the clinic while I try to find her a good home."

"Which won't be easy."

"Not for a pregnant dog, no," Sara admitted. She caught the compassionate look in his eyes and hid a smile. She already knew where this was heading and it gave her a tentative sense of relief.

"Of course, the clinic isn't ideal for her," she added somberly. "With all of the stress of the other dogs barking at every sound and strangers around her all day. Poor thing. Not good for the puppies, either."

"Maybe you could leave her here. With me."

Sara frowned. "Just as a loose stray, you mean? I really can't—"

"No. As…as…my own dog."

She caught the slight hesitation in his voice. "If you don't *really* want to give her a permanent, loving home, I won't leave her here. It's a commitment for her lifetime, you know."

"Right."

"You said you weren't going to stay in Montana for very long. What will happen to her then?"

He seemed to give that a moment's thought, then nodded decisively. "She'll come with me. I haven't had a travel buddy with me for years, and I think she'll be exactly right."

"I usually don't like taking people up on their snap decisions. I can keep her for you, if you want to think about this for a week or so."

"Not necessary. And you don't have a good space for her and her pups right now, anyway. Right? I can fix a warm bed for her in the house."

"I have no idea if she's been housebroken. I'd guess not."

"I'll work with her."

Sara bit her lower lip. "Promise you'll give her back to me if you change your mind?"

"That won't happen. What about her vet care? Do you know if she's up to date on everything?"

"If you'd seen where she came from, you wouldn't even ask."

"So where do I start?"

"Gestation averages right around two months. At thirty-five days I usually recommend putting a pregnant dog on dry puppy food for its extra nutrition, about twice the amount of food she would usually have." Sara eyed Lucy thoughtfully. "I don't know exactly how many days along she is, but she's obviously getting close and she's undernourished. Can you get into town soon? The feed mill or grocery store might carry it, though what we have at the clinic is a lot better and more expensive. She'll need to be on it until she stops nursing."

"Of course."

"While you're in town, you can pick up some wormer too. We usually deworm ten days before whelping, then every three weeks while the dog is still nursing."

"Shots?"

"We need to wait on her vaccinations until after the pups arrive. There's no risk for them at that point." His concern about Lucy's welfare was reassuring, and she knew she'd made the right choice leaving Lucy in his care. She knelt down and ran her hands over Lucy's swollen flanks. "Since her history is pretty sketchy, you might also want her to have a postnatal exam and have the pups examined, as well. I could come back out, or you could bring them to the clinic."

"Gotcha. Anything else?"

"Check the clinic website and print off our flyer on raising puppies." She picked up her satchel. "If she has any problems, or you have any questions, just call. Oh— and take off that choke collar she's been wearing and get her a nylon web or leather collar with a buckle."

"I will. Thanks."

about Devlin's dog?"

lives with Uncle Devlin." Bella pouted. "She's And she's really, *really big*."

uld give a puppy to Uncle Devlin so Daisy has nd then keep the rest!" Sophie beamed. "Right? ndma Betty could have a friend too."

idea." Tate grinned at them, charmed as always earnest appeals. "I'm sure Dev and Grandma e that."

grandma had been too much of a mouthful for ay when they first came to the ranch, so to them yone else, Betty was simply grandma.

ou have any idea of the trouble you're causing? le. We'll never hear the end of this." Jess leveled ok at Tate. "And as your older and much wiser I just have to ask. Does this mean you're ready down and stay home? It won't be easy traveling s year-around with a dog."

won't be a problem. And yes, I'm still planning on. I'll always need new towns ahead and the old ny rearview mirror."

raised her eyebrows. "So apparently the match heaven that Jess and Dev told me about…"

r existed. Sara and I were in the same high school iends from long ago. Only that." And if he kept imself that, maybe he would even believe it…in two or three.

you two dated. Right?"

hot a quelling glance at Jess. "Maybe for just a le, senior year in high school. But it wasn't seri- a had…ulterior motives that didn't work out, and ended it. Which was fine with me. Case closed."

rior *what*?" Abby looked between Jess and Tate. oes that mean?"

He held on to the dog when Sara headed for her truck. When she glanced in the rearview mirror as she drove away, he was kneeling beside Lucy and stroking her ragged coat.

Sara felt her heart warm at the gentleness she remembered so well.

As a senior she'd tried to distract her parents by dating the wildest boy in town—hoping they would finally stop fighting and stop threatening each other with divorce if they were worried about *her* for once.

The wild and irresponsible son of the county's richest rancher, Tate had been the perfect choice, but he was one of the coolest kids in high school and she hadn't been one of the pretty, popular girls. Studious, shy and awkward, she'd fumbled over her words more often than not.

Even her best friends had told her she was crazy, but still she'd gathered her courage, tried to emulate the popular girls and shyly flirted with him.

To her utter amazement he actually asked her out, and during the following months she'd found more depth, kindness and character in him than she'd ever thought possible given his reputation.

But her stupid plan failed.

Her parents split anyway—for the third time. And her guilt had grown.

She'd been a fraud. A liar. She'd tried to use someone who deserved far, far better.

And in the process she'd developed the world's biggest crush on a boy who could learn the truth about her plan at any moment from any one of her so-called friends… and then he'd never believe that she really and truly cared. That she *loved* him.

She'd drowned in misery before finally blurting out the truth, knowing that he had trusted her, cared about her—and that what she had done was unforgivable. She'd deceived him, and along the way, had deceived herself.

He'd stared at her for a long moment. Then he'd walked away as if she'd meant nothing, and her heart had broken into a thousand pieces.

Seeing him at school the next day with other girls fawning all over him had poured acid on her broken heart until she thought she would die. But it taught her a good lesson.

Loving someone—*commitment*—wasn't something she'd dared risk.

Courtesy of her parents, she'd seen how miserable marriage could be, how infidelities and lies could tear a family apart, how forgiveness and second chances just led to even more pain in the future.

And losing someone she loved was more painful than she could bear.

So she'd turned to what mattered most to her parents. The accomplishments that proved her worth, the tangible evidence of success.

A bachelor's.

Master's.

And then a professional degree—though she'd rebelled and defiantly gone her own route, on that score.

Tate had clearly grown up to be a kind and caring person, and it would be far too easy to fall for him all over again. But there was no point in letting her imagination run wild where he was concerned.

She already knew how easy it was to love him. How easily it could all end. She would need to guard her heart well or it would be broken all over again.

Jess burst out laughing over supper at the main ranch house a few hours later. "You did *what*?"

"Adopted a dog," Tate repeated. "Have a proble
that?"

"No. Not at all. I just never thought I'd see Mr. F
and Fancy-Free taking on any kind of responsibil
even for a dog. You've always said that you wan
lutely nothing to tie you down. Ever."

Tate glared at him over the rim of his co
"I'm now realizing just how peaceful my life
I moved back."

"You and Dev can even compare notes, bec
Chloe adopted a stray last summer." Jess's gr
"And now you'll soon have puppies on your
the looks of things, a bumper crop. Fun."

Jess and Abby's adopted seven-year-old t
and Bella, looked at each other and bounc
their chairs. "We want them. We could k
Uncle Tate! We got lotsa room."

Jess and Abby had taken the girls
mother—Jess's troubled cousin—hadn't b
for them, and he could see that the twins a
wrapped around their little fingers.

"Sounds like a good idea to me, girls
triumphant grin at him as Jess's own gr

"Whoa," Abby said, barely suppress
holding her hands up. "That's somethi
later. You already have a puppy. Reme

"But Poofy is a big dog now," Bella
arms stubbornly across her chest.

A big dog indeed. At the sound of
old golden retriever mix lumbered to
the kitchen to rest his head on her lap
least eighty or ninety pounds.

"He's not a fluffy puppy anymore
to play with," Sophie added. "Lots.

Jess shrugged.

Tate took his plate to the sink, rinsed it and put it in the dishwasher, then headed for the door. "Thanks for a wonderful meal, Abby. Tell Grandma Betty that I loved her apple pie and missed seeing her tonight. I hope she had fun at bingo."

He slipped out the back door and headed for his pickup, glad to be outside and away from the gentle teasing and probing questions that flew across the table every time he joined Jess and his family for supper.

He knew it all stemmed from love and caring, the kind of camaraderie he was blessed to still have despite all of his years away.

But he wasn't ready to discuss his past with Sara. Not with anyone. He'd been such a fool.

Their relationship as high school seniors had started out as just a ruse she'd planned, an attempt at a goal that had nothing to do with him.

Unaware of it, he'd been overcome with the heady emotions of an adolescent crush that had nearly destroyed him when he learned the truth. He'd fallen in love with her. She'd never felt the same. And at the end, it took all of his courage to shrug and walk away as if none of it mattered.

He suspected those wounds were with him still…silently warning him whenever a new romance turned a little too serious.

So *what* had come over him during Sara's vet call? He'd seen many a stray dog over the years. Caught them and took them to no-kill shelters, whenever he could, or found a buddy who wanted a family dog.

But Jess knew him too well, and he was right. Tate had never, ever wanted to take on the responsibility of anyone or anything himself—not even a dog—which would just make his traveling life more difficult.

And yet, he'd taken one look at Lucy and he'd felt surprising warmth expand in his chest. He hadn't been able to look away from the sadness in her eyes and drooping ears, or the way she seemed to cower with her head lowered, her tail feebly, almost imperceptibly wagging, as if she was still holding on to a thread of hope that someone might take her in. He'd never been so sure that a dog was his destiny.

Lucy had stirred in him an unfamiliar rush of protectiveness. Within minutes of seeing her, he'd known that he just couldn't let Sara take her away.

After Sara left for another ranch call, he'd gone straight to town for the wormer and special puppy food at the clinic, then he'd come home to build a whelping box thickly padded with newspapers and a folded wool blanket.

Back when his rodeo buddy Jace got married he'd thought about settling down, as well, but he'd given up finding the right woman long ago.

Was his abrupt change of heart over Lucy—his unexpected new companion—a small sign that his life was going to change?

Foolish thought.

He gave a short, self-deprecating laugh as he drove home to the old Branson place.

The only big change in his future would be when he began his new career as a rodeo contractor. And that was just fine with him. Who could ask for anything more?

Seeing old friends at the rodeos. Travel. Excitement. A new town every week. It was a perfect life.

Or was it?

Chapter Three

Tate slowed his mare to a walk as he entered the pine forest and twisted in the saddle to survey the fence line.

Like most snowfalls this time of year, much of the five inches yesterday was already melting in the brittle February sunshine and there were exposed patches of winter-dried grass in the meadows. This far up in the foothills, the snow was still deep in the shade of the pines—not yet the ideal weather for riding the fence to check for damage. But with the rodeo contractor's auction coming up in Colorado the first weekend in May, he needed to make use of every minute, to stay ahead of chores. Knowing the locations and extent of any repairs would help him hit the ground running after the spring thaw.

Blondie lowered her head as she carefully picked her way past a fallen tree, jerking to a halt with a loud snort at the sudden frenzied motion of a rabbit bounding from its hiding place beneath the snow-blanketed branches.

Tate reached forward to rest a steadying hand on her neck. "Good girl," he murmured. "Take it easy."

He had a dozen horses back in the barn, mostly two-year-olds he was starting under saddle in the indoor arena for Jess. Any one of them might have panicked and shied violently.

But Blondie was a big solid three-year-old mare Jess had started late last year and she showed a fair level of common sense. If Tate had any plans to stick around, he'd want to keep her. But he wasn't staying, and with her deep palomino color and pretty head, she would bring a good price at auction later this year…once he'd put more ranch work experience on her odometer.

Over the next rise he again paused to study the fencing for downed or loose wire, noting several leaning fence posts that would need replacement after the spring thaw.

Alarm rushed through him at the faint scent of wood smoke drifting on the crisp mountain air. *Fire?*

There were no resorts up here, no year-around homes he could recall, that lay beyond this northern boundary of Langford-owned property and might be running a wood furnace. The moisture-laden ground meant there was minimal chance of wildfires this time of year. *But still…*

From somewhere beyond the trees he heard a dog start to bark. Standing in his stirrups, he leaned forward and scanned the dense timber.

When he reached the fence he could barely make out the frame of the old, abandoned cabin he remembered from years back, no more than fifty yards away and nearly obscured by trees and brush. He did a double-take at the gleaming dark green steel roof, and the smoke curling up from its chimney. It was inhabited now?

The barking grew louder, then a small, shaggy dog bounded through the brush and headed straight for the fence. In a flash it was under Blondie's hooves, yapping and racing in circles in the snow.

The scared rabbit had been one thing, but a dog in attack mode—however small—was another. The mare reared and violently pivoted before Tate could stop her, slamming his knee against a tree and sending a lightning bolt of pain up his leg.

She scrambled to regain her footing in the deep snow, her weight first pinning him, then scraping his leg against the rough bark.

The dog backed a few yards away but continued its insane barking, sending Blondie dancing sideways.

"Susie! Here, Susie!" From the vicinity of the cabin someone started whistling, then shouting again.

A totally unexpected but all-too-familiar voice.

A moment later, Sara stumbled through the brush and reached the fence, her red stocking cap askew and puffy red jacket unzipped.

"I'm so, so sorry!" she called out as she eyed the fence, moved to a section where the barbwire sagged and carefully slipped between the strands to scoop up the little dog.

Her eyes widened and her cheeks turned rosy when she finally looked up at him. "*Tate?* What are you doing way up here?"

Blondie settled down now that the little beast was contained. He shook some slack in the reins. "Riding fence."

Sara eyed the snow that almost reached her knees in this pine-shaded area. "Now? This time of year?"

"I'm just figuring out how much needs to be done." He shifted in the saddle to ease his aching knee. "We'll be moving cattle up here in the spring."

The dog wiggled in her arms, clearly ready to do battle again. Sara readjusted her grip. "How's Lucy? Has she had her pups yet?"

"Nope. But I fixed a whelping box for her in a quiet corner of the kitchen, where the pups will be warm enough. I think it's going to be soon. I'm not sure the poor thing can get any bigger."

Sara grinned. "You know what signs to watch for, right? Did you print off that flyer on the website?"

He nodded. "We also had a number of litters on the ranch. Dad raised blue heelers for years."

He lifted his gaze toward the cabin. "That place was empty, back when I was growing up. I didn't know anyone was living way out there."

Her expression cooled. "You wouldn't. You and I were away at college when your father stole my aunt and uncle's ranch."

"I'm not sure *stole* is the right—" He'd instinctively started to defend Dad, but bit back the words. She was probably right.

Dad had always been proud of the strings he pulled for his own benefit, and the deals he wrangled without regard for anyone who might be hurt. He'd often bragged about those "deals" over the supper table, affirming that *this* was the way a man succeeded in life.

Did the locals now regret the return of his sons, assuming that all three had that same streak of avarice? Lack of compassion?

"That cabin is the place my aunt and uncle bought after their foreclosure," Sara continued. "It was in bad shape, but Warren is—or was—a skilled craftsman, and they both worked hard to make it livable again. Then his health started to fail, and they had no choice. They had to move into town. It's been empty for over a year, but I'm living there now."

Tate surveyed the western horizon, where he could see the majestic snow-covered peaks of the Rockies through the pines. "They couldn't find a buyer? This is a beautiful location."

"They should have," she shot back, her voice trembling with emotion. "They needed the money then, and need it even more now. But they stubbornly held on to it. They know how much I love this part of the Rockies, and insisted they wanted it to be my legacy."

"Good people." He regarded her somberly, wondering if his own father had ever done such a selfless thing in his life. Not likely.

After Heather's death at the age of four, Dad had readily placed the blame on his young sons' carelessness, rather than own up to what he'd done to their sister. Accident or not, Dad had typically thought only to protect his own pride and reputation, with no regard for the emotional scars his fabrication caused his boys.

By mutual, unspoken agreement, the brothers had never again discussed it—a scar had to be better than a raw, open wound.

Had Jess and Devlin made peace with Dad over what happened? Forgiven him? Tate had no idea. But Dad had been especially hard on them, to the point of cruelty, and that was something Tate could never forgive.

They hadn't deserved to take the blame. He had. But at the age of six he'd been too scared to face his father's rage, and the other two hadn't let him try.

"Warren and Millie have tried to refuse, but I'm gradually paying them every penny the property is worth, to build up their savings again," Sara continued. "The minute I heard about the Pine Bend clinic coming up for sale, I knew my prayers had been answered. Now I live close enough to watch over them and help in any way I can."

In high school, Tate had imagined her to be a spoiled rich girl, as the only child of two physicians who worked at the clinic in town. Even when they dated during their senior year, she'd been carefully circumspect about her family life, while he'd been a callow, self-centered teen who didn't think to ask.

But now he wondered. Where had her parents been through all of the hardship Warren and Millie had endured? Had they not thought to help out? And why had this aunt and uncle practically raised Sara?

But it wasn't his business to ask, and he suspected the Langfords weren't the only dysfunctional family in the county.

"So…how do you like living way back here? It has to be sort of lonely, right?"

Her blue eyes sparkled with humor. "Well…I'm not *exactly* alone."

His assumption and her vague reply left them with a long, awkward pause.

He hadn't given a thought to the fact that she was probably married, but of course she was—or she had someone in her life. A pretty gal like her with that shimmering waterfall of pale blond hair would turn heads wherever she went, and she was also smart and successful, with DVM behind her name.

"I can introduce you to the 'family,' if that horse will tie."

He blinked, and felt his heart stumble. *Family?*

There were certainly no emotional connections left between them, after all these years, yet he found himself hesitating to meet whoever it was who had captured Sara's heart. Did he even know how lucky he was?

An excuse nearly tumbled from his lips. *Sorry—too busy. I've got to get back to work.*

But he was his own boss. Sara knew full well that he didn't punch a clock. And he'd left Blondie's halter under the bridle when he saddled her this morning, in case he needed to stop somewhere and tie her, so he hardly had that excuse, either. "Uh…sure."

Gingerly dismounting to avoid too much weight on his

throbbing knee, he grabbed the heavy cotton lead rope draped over the saddle horn, snapped it to the halter and tied the mare to a sturdy tree with a quick-release safety knot.

He limped after Sara as she headed for the log cabin with the little dog in her arms. With a final glance back at Blondie, he followed her through the trees, past a small corral and shed, and up onto the covered porch, surprised at seeing an attached garage—obviously newer—at the far end of the cabin.

Sara looked over her shoulder at him before pushing the door open. "What happened to your leg?"

"It's nothing."

"No, really—you definitely weren't limping when I stopped by to look at your gelding on Thursday. Wait— is that *blood*?"

He glanced down at the long vertical tear at the side of his knee and a dark stain dampening the denim. "It's nothing. I'll take care of it later on."

She rolled her eyes at that. "I forgot. You're a tough guy. You rodeoed for how many years? I suppose you were always limping home with one injury or another."

"Actually, it wasn't all that often," he said dryly. "The whole point was to stay aboard and *not* get hurt—or I would've quit years ago."

"Come on in. If you start to bleed more, I promise I can do something about it." She tilted her head toward the interior of the house. "This might be a bit alarming at first, so just be prepared. I promise none of them bite."

None of them? He followed her through the door and paused, letting his eyes adjust to the gloom. Something in here could *bite*?

She flipped a wall switch, lighting a large antler chandelier hanging from the center of the high, pitched ceiling.

Wings flapped.

Something emitted an earsplitting screech. Several dogs growled.

From across the room he felt the golden, glowing stare of what appeared to be a very large creature—possibly a pony—lurking in the shadows. A Newfoundland, he realized, when it took a wary move forward into the light.

Before he could take a second step inside, he felt a river of five meowing cats winding around his ankles.

"This is why I couldn't bring a pregnant dog home with me." Sara put Susie down and watched her scamper away. "I've got too many animals here already. The stress on Lucy and her pups would have been too much for them."

He blinked, taking it all in. "So…you've adopted them *all*?"

"Goodness no. Every animal here is a hard-luck case of some kind. Injured, abandoned, strays or owner surrenders, and most need some degree of rehab. In a month or so they'll be ready to go and will hopefully find good homes via the no-kill shelter in the next county." She crossed the great room to the open-concept kitchen, where she began filling various sizes of stainless-steel food dishes. "But just like the day I happened to find Lucy, the need never really goes away."

On the railing of an open loft at the back of the cabin, something large moved in the shadows. It moved again and he realized it was an enormous bird perched in the darkness. It spread its wings, flapped them, then it marched sideways a few steps.

Back, and forth.

Back, and forth.

An eerie, almost electronic voice began rapping out a familiar song.

A *parrot*? Even from here, its massive beak and powerful claws appeared capable of decimating a two-by-four.

He surveyed the rest of the animals, then looked up at the parrot again as his realization dawned. "So this is the family you mentioned?"

Sara followed his gaze and nodded. "In a manner of speaking, anyway. That's Theodore. I hope you liked the music from the Broadway show *Hamilton*."

"Huh?"

"Theo's owner had to go to a nursing home. She was the sweetest elderly lady, who loved what she called the *peppy beat* of the show's rap songs. She played the CD all the time, and Theodore knows at least part of every song. Every. Last. Song. And I'm not kidding."

"He's…exceptionally good."

"I actually love the music—I even got to see one of the shows in Chicago. But unfortunately, his proclivity for entertaining is going to make him difficult to rehome, unless I can find him a new owner with hearing loss or one who loves that show."

"Can't you keep him?"

"The hardest part of trying to rehab and rehome animals is giving them up. But if I didn't—" she lifted a shoulder in a slight shrug "—then I would run out of room for the next ones in need."

Tate stepped farther into the great room, mindful of the cats underfoot. If Sara had told him about the number of furred and feathered residents in her cabin, he would have expected clutter and cages everywhere.

But the cabin smelled faintly of lemon furniture polish and the bouquet of flowers on the round oak kitchen table, and everywhere he looked, the place was neat and clean. And now that he looked a little closer, he gave a long, low whistle.

The kitchen had been fitted with high-end cabinetry that must have been custom-made. The burnished hickory wood flooring, with its light and dark tones, gave the place an airy feel, and three of the exterior walls were filled with large multipaned windows that seemed to make the surrounding forest a continuation of the living space. "This is beautiful," he murmured as his gaze fell on the stone fireplace at one end of the great room. "I had no idea."

Sara laughed. "It was a shambles until Warren and Millie moved here. Roof half gone, rotted flooring. Home to chipmunks and squirrels, and I doubt even the creatures were impressed."

"How did they find the right craftsmen in these parts?"

"Warren was a lifelong rancher, but one of his favorite TV channels is HGTV. Between YouTube, the internet and the library, he taught himself and he did it all—except the steel roof. He made the handcrafted cabinets, laid the wood floors, even did the stonework around the fireplace."

Tate whistled under his breath. "It must have been hard to leave this behind."

"It broke his heart, honestly, and Millie's too. But after he had some small strokes, this place was just too remote for driving into town for doctors' appointments and groceries—especially in bad weather." Sara gestured toward one of several barstools lined up along the kitchen island. "Take a seat and let me look at your wound."

"No need. I really do need to get going." The wound didn't hurt much and it didn't seem to be bleeding now, but the knee itself was starting to throb. The longer he lingered, the harder it would be to get back on Blondie and manage the nearly two-hour ride home. "I'll take care of it later."

She gave him a stern look. "Just humor me, okay? It won't take but a minute. Sit."

With a sigh he followed her directions and let her prop his injured leg on a step stool. The tear in the denim was maybe ten inches or so, allowing ample access. "Bled a little more than I realized," he muttered, looking at the wide area of deep abrasion surrounding a long narrow gash. "But looks like it stopped. No worries."

She held up a forefinger. *"Stay."*

Amused, he did as he was told. This was definitely a woman who spent a lot of time talking to animals. And with that no-nonsense tone of hers, they probably instantly obeyed.

She reached for a plastic storage box on the counter and withdrew disposable gloves, a package of four-by-four sterile gauze squares, a tube of antibiotic cream and a stainless-steel bowl that she filled with warm water.

"The laceration is long but shallow, and it isn't gaping, so I don't believe you need stitches," she murmured as she began cleaning the wound with a series of fresh gauze squares soaked in water. "But go see your doc if you want a second opinion. My human first-aid info is all from a medical site on the internet."

"Nope. This isn't much more than a scratch and a scrape."

She pinned him with a stern look. "You *really* need to go if you aren't up to date on your tetanus vaccine. Do you remember the date of your last one?"

"Six months."

"Good. When you get home you might want to take a long hot shower and rinse it again for a good five minutes, then re-dress the wound with antibiotic cream and cover with gauze."

"Thanks. Can you add this to my vet bill?"

"I'd have a pretty hard time explaining it to my licensing board." She laughed. "So that's a no. You do know you shouldn't use peroxide, Mercurochrome or alcohol on this, right? Not necessary, painful and they delay healing, from what I've read online about human injuries. But again—check with your doctor."

"Yes, ma'am."

"This will get you home, at least, without your jeans abrading the wound and making it worse."

The moment was anything but intimate, yet he found himself transfixed by her intense concentration and the gentle touch of her fingertips as she deftly patted the wound dry with clean gauze squares and applied the antibiotic cream. She surveyed her handiwork, then covered the area with fresh gauze that she held in place with medical adhesive tape.

"Best keep the area covered and moist with an antibiotic cream for a few days, then you could switch to something like Vaseline for a couple days if you want." She glanced up at him, but her gaze abruptly veered away. A hint of pink touched her cheekbones. "Um…it'll heal better if the wound doesn't get too dry."

"Thanks." He watched her finish, then looked up at her with a grin. "You sure have a good bedside manner. You would have been a fine doc—"

"I *am* a doctor." Her smile dissolved. "Of veterinary medicine."

Chagrined, he held up his hands. "Sorry. That didn't come out quite right."

"I got *way* too much of that from my parents."

"Where are they now?"

"They finally became involved in a church, reconciled and found their calling as medical missionaries in Africa. Ironic, really, since I don't think they'll ever forgive me for defying them."

"Pardon me for saying so, but that doesn't seem fair."

She stowed away her supplies and carried the bowl of water to the kitchen sink. "They had my whole career planned out for me, right down to the medical school I would attend, and how I would work with them. It's all they talked about, when they pushed me to do better in school. When I was younger, all I cared about was pleasing them, so I was on board."

"What happened?"

"I realized that I didn't want to be like them, tied to a health clinic with back-to-back appointments all day. Working in their shadow. Instead, now I have a fantastic variety—ortho, OB, surgeries and I get to sort out complex medical problems. Sometimes all in the same day."

"All the greater challenge since your patients can't talk. Right?"

She sent a sharp glance over her shoulder, as if deciding whether or not he was mocking her. "True. And I like splitting time between ranch calls and the clinic—the chance to be outside. I'd rather have my career than anything else in the world."

"I do understand. It was Jess's dream too. He talked about it from grade school on."

Wishing he'd managed to keep his mouth shut and not insult her, Tate stood and lifted a hand to rest it on her shoulder in apology, but let it drop to his side. There'd been a time in high school when he could've drawn her into an embrace, but those days were long gone.

She wouldn't welcome that intimacy now.

At the door of her cabin he shouldered on his jacket and snagged his Stetson from a hook on the wall. "I'm proud of you, Sara. You absolutely made the right choice. And don't let anyone tell you any different."

But from the distant expression in her eyes, he knew she didn't believe him.

* * *

Langford? Sara did a double take at the name on the revised schedule in her hand, then looked up at the clock, her heart picking up a momentary erratic beat.

Mondays, Wednesdays and Friday afternoons were—barring emergency ranch calls—set aside for small-animal-clinic appointments, but the time slot at one o'clock had been open when she'd left for an emergency colic case out in the country. "This name written in—I can't quite read it."

Neta—the seventysomething receptionist who had been working at the clinic since the dawn of time—glanced up from the stacks of billing statements and envelopes on her desk. "Tate Langford. He's bringing in a litter of pups and their mom. I told him to come at one, because there won't be any other clients and their animals coming in until after two. Anna just finished sanitizing the first exam room."

"Good thinking. No sense exposing those young pups to anything." Tires crunched to a halt in front of the building and they both looked toward the wall of windows facing the highway.

"Looks like one of the Langford pickups—so that must be him. *Anna!*" Neta bellowed over her shoulder. "Got a client out front needing some help."

"I think she's running some blood chemistries for me. I'll go." Sara folded the schedule and dropped it into a pocket of her lab coat on her way to the front door.

Outside, a brisk February breeze laden with a promise of snow sent a shiver down her back as she reached the side of the gleaming black Dodge pickup.

Tate opened the back door on the driver's side and reached for a large cardboard box reinforced with duct tape on the sides and bottom. Lucy danced at his side, clearly agitated over the welfare of her pups and trying to catch a glimpse of them.

"Hey, Tate. Looks like you have your hands full. I can take Lucy."

"Thanks." He shot a quick glance at her over his shoulder and handed her the leash, then turned back to drape a folded blanket over the top of the box. "They were born late Sunday night. I debated about bringing them into town today, since they're so young. But I expect my two little nieces will be visiting them often, so Lucy needs her health exam and vaccinations."

"They'll be fine. They won't be in contact with any other dogs right now, and this won't take long. But if you can, hold the girls off for a couple weeks until the puppies are a bit older."

"While I'm here, I also want to make sure the pups are all right. It doesn't sound like their mom had the best care." Tate hefted the box of puppies into his arms and nudged the truck door shut with his shoulder, then locked it with a valet key. "I'm leaving the truck running so it stays warm enough inside."

He followed Sara into the exam room, where he lifted off the blanket and put the box on the floor so Lucy could snuffle through the mewling litter, performing her own inspection. "Look at 'em. Not sure what happened here, but there are six and none of them even *look* related," he said with a low laugh. "It won't be hard to tell them apart."

Sara stepped out into the hallway. "Anna—can you come in, please?"

Lucy watched anxiously as Sara weighed and examined each pup, and took its temp while the vet tech jotted down careful notes.

Sara looked up at Tate as she settled the final pup among

its siblings. The six squealing pups blindly squirmed over each other, until they were back into a warm pile.

"They all look normal and healthy. No cleft palates. The black-and-white female is a couple ounces less than the others, though, so you'll need to keep an eye on her. Do you have a digital kitchen or postal scale?"

"Uh…no. But I'll see if I can find one in town—or order online."

"Good. It wouldn't hurt to weigh all of them every day or two to make sure they are steadily growing—especially the smallest one. If she doesn't catch up, she'll need supplemental feedings."

"This all sounds like being a new dad." The slash of a dimple in Tate's cheek deepened with his wry smile. "Not that I'll ever know. What else do I need to do?"

She glanced up at him, trying to hide her surprise at his casual dismissal of ever having a family.

Tate had always had a reputation among the girls in town as a charming, handsome guy with a sideways glance and quicksilver grin that could send any girl's heart into overdrive. The years had only added to that masculine appeal, so surely he would've had no end of opportunities to settle down by now.

So what had happened? Had he turned into the kind of guy who left a trail of broken hearts in his wake and didn't care?

She reined in her errant thoughts and tried to remember what she was going to say. "Um…if you want, I can send some puppy formula home with you, just in case. It could save another trip to town if you need it. Otherwise you can return it."

"Great idea."

"About the other things to remember, deworm the pups at three or four weeks, and again three weeks later—when they receive their first vaccinations. Heartworm meds will start in the spring."

"I think I should've been writing all of this down," he said with a rueful shake of his head.

"No worries—I'll ask Neta to send you postcard reminders, or texts if you prefer."

"Texts, please. Is there anything else I need to know?"

Sara studied Lucy's colorful family. "Basically, plump, contented puppies are a good sign that all is well. For the first couple weeks they'll mostly be quiet—just sleeping or eating. But if any of them seem more restless than the others and vocalize more, they might be too cold or not getting enough to eat. Sometimes a smaller one won't compete well enough with its littermates. How warm is your kitchen?"

"Drafty," Tate admitted as he partially covered the box again so Lucy could still keep an eye on her family. "But I do have a heat lamp hanging over their box so it's a steady eighty-five degrees in there, and three of the sides are high. I read about doing that on your clinic website. Am I right?"

"Exactly—for the first four days. Then gradually lower to eighty during the next six days. After that, they should be able to regulate their body temps better, so seventy-two degrees through week four is fine."

He nodded. "And weaning?"

"They can be completely weaned at six weeks, but it's important to keep the litter together another two weeks for their social development. We can talk about starting puppy food and weaning later on."

Sara lifted Lucy onto the stainless-steel exam table and administered her vaccinations, then withdrew a blood sample that Anna took to the lab. "I'm running a heartworm test. The risk is pretty low in this part of Montana, but there are still some cases every year and it can be fatal. So I need to be sure."

"What then?"

"If she's negative, a monthly heartworm prevention med, May through October. If she's positive, she would definitely need to be treated."

Anna popped back into the room with a smile and a thumbs-up, her long russet ponytail swinging. "Negative."

"Good news." Sara began her examination, calling out to Anna the details to be recorded.

When the exam was complete, Anna scooped Lucy from the table and set her on the floor next to the box of puppies. "Do you want me to get some formula from the storeroom?"

"Please. Just put it on the front counter." Sara bent down to cradle Lucy's head between her hands. "Such a sweet dog."

"So she's okay?"

Sara straightened. "She's underweight, but that was obvious from the start. Otherwise she's actually in pretty good shape, all things considered. And from the looks of the pups, she's feeding them well."

"Mighty glad to hear it. What do I owe you today?"

"Neta will figure it out and add it to your bill since I have an appointment next week to check that injured colt and vaccinate your barn cats." Sara took Lucy's leash while Tate shouldered on his jacket and tucked the blanket over the box of puppies. "So how is that leg of yours? You're barely limping."

He grinned at her. "I've had five days to heal, and my veterinarian did a great job."

"No, really—did you have a doctor take a look at it?"

He laughed. "A guy doesn't rodeo for years and go to a doctor for a scratch. He'd be laughed right off the circuit."

"But it wasn't just a scratch. On Saturday, you were limping as if that knee joint was really painful."

"Yeah…well. It's been banged up a few times over the years. Surgery twice. But I iced it that night and took ibuprofen through the weekend. It's fine."

She bit her lower lip. "If my wayward dog had anything to do with you getting hurt, I'm truly sorry. I took her outside to potty and she got away from me. I heard her barking but I couldn't catch up in time. I feel like I owe you. A dinner, or…something. Cookies? Would a weekly supply of cookies do?"

"No need." He shrugged off her concern and picked up the puppy box. "She gave the mare a little lesson on dogs, so it was all good."

On her way out the door Sara grabbed the puppy formula, then followed Tate to his truck. "Goodness—I think the breeze has picked up and the temperature has dropped a good ten degrees."

Once Tate had placed the box of puppies in the backseat, he lifted Lucy in next to them and shut the door.

"Thanks, Sara." He raised a hand as if to shake hers, then dropped it with a low laugh. "Seems strange, being so formal. But I guess we hardly know each other anymore. Maybe dinner would be nice sometime—just to catch up."

"Uh…yes. Sometime." She took a step back and wrapped her hands around her middle to ward off the chill, wishing she hadn't made that suggestion about dinner. Polite distance, she could handle. But superficial chitchat over dinner sounded awkward, even uncomfortable, unless more people were there to fill any conversational voids. "I—I'll see you out at the ranch next Thursday. Don't forget to catch your cats before I get there."

"A cat rodeo. My specialty."

His silvery eyes twinkled with humor and for just that

moment, she felt herself falling under the spell of his trademark Langford charm.

But more than a few failed romances had taught her how foolish she'd been to fall for guys who inevitably just walked away.

And no one, not even her old high school crush, could tempt her to make that mistake again.

Chapter Four

The next morning, Sara parked her vet truck in front of the two-story Pine Bend Apartment building, wrapped a scarf around her neck and trudged up the long, snow-covered walkway to the front door.

The caretaker was just starting to remove the latest five inches of snow with a noisy snowblower, and he returned her nod of greeting as she passed. "They're home," he shouted over the din. "Haven't been out all day."

She murmured a small prayer of thanks as she stepped inside the building and stamped the snow from her boots.

This wasn't Warren and Millie's nice, cozy cabin. Certainly not the Ritz, with its fading 1970s decor. The senior condos across town were far nicer. But at least the entryway and halls here were warm, and there were maintenance folks to keep the walks and parking lot cleared. They knew the residents well and even knew most of the guests who came and went, which added a layer of safety.

And now, the home health aides could come three times a week instead of just once, since Millie and Warren were just blocks away from the health center.

For all that the place lacked in grandeur, it offered far more safety and assistance for an elderly couple than their isolated cabin two miles up a torturous road into the foothills, where phone reception was poor and no one could easily check on them.

Their apartment door was ajar, in silent anticipation of her visit. "Hi there, anyone home?"

The cramped main-floor apartment consisted of a living room, two small bedrooms, a tiny kitchenette and a bathroom. She could hear the television was off, and had no doubt that Warren had been in his favorite chair at the window, watching for her to arrive for the last half hour or more.

Slippered feet shuffled toward the door. "Sara?"

Warren pulled the door open wide, his gaunt, angular frame bent over his grip on a cane. "I thought I saw your truck out in front. How are the roads?"

She shifted the handles of her two denim shopping bags to her other arm and gave him a quick hug. "Not bad. We're supposed to have sunshine and temps in the forties tomorrow, so it will all melt just in time for your doctor's appointment. How are you feeling today?"

He shrugged. Looked away. "Fine."

"You would say fine no matter what, Uncle Warren," she teased, hiding her concern about his labored breathing and sallow complexion. "Go sit down and get your oxygen cannula back in place, and I'll put away these groceries."

With his emphysema, diabetes, heart disease and history of strokes, he was on Sara's mind all the time, but he was too stubborn to accept much help, follow his diet or even regularly take all the meds he was supposed to.

Millie constantly fluttered about him, trying to get him to take better care of himself, but he'd resisted her efforts and had aged far beyond his years. That he was still walking around outside a nursing home could only be an answer to Sara's and Millie's prayers.

"Have you been using your oxygen?"

He tilted his head toward the tank by his chair and the loops of tubing at its base. "When I sit. I don't like dragging that tangle all over the place, where your aunt or I might trip."

Sara took the groceries to the kitchen and began putting everything away, then started browning some ground beef and chopped onion in a skillet. "Is she still napping?"

"She didn't sleep too well last night, but I 'spect she'll be out any minute now."

He settled into his recliner and swiveled it so he could see the kitchen. "Sure smells good."

"I have another forty-five minutes before my afternoon appointments, so I thought I'd start a quick batch of chili and put it in the slow cooker on High. It should be ready by your six o'clock news show."

Millie, a fragile little sprite barely five feet tall, stepped out of the bedroom and came over to give Sara a hug. "Well, my goodness sakes. You didn't need to go to all that trouble for us, dear."

Sara gave her a kiss on her wrinkled cheek. "It's no trouble. I like to cook, but it's just me and a lot of animals at the cabin. Can I make you two some coffee, and something for lunch?"

"I can do that," Millie protested. "The senior meals driver brought us so much yesterday that I told them to skip us today. Will you join us?"

"I've already had something, but thanks." A noon meal from yesterday, stretched for two days, couldn't possibly be enough for just the two of them. "Honestly, you two should eat everything they send you, the same day it arrives. Remember when you used to tell me to be part of the 'clean plate club' when I was a kid?"

Millie chuckled as she bustled about filling the coffee maker, then patted Sara's arm and smiled sadly.

With her aunt's abrupt change of expression, Sara braced herself. She knew what was coming next.

"It just isn't right that a sweet girl like you is all alone. You know, there's the nicest young man at church every Sunday. Have you seen him? A little heavy. Glasses. Very shy. He lives with his mother, at the south end of Main, and I hear he is very good to her. That's always a sign of character."

Sara tried not to roll her eyes at the ongoing saga of *The Available Young Men of Pine Bend*. Every time she saw Millie, there was another prospect.

"I'm not interested. Not in anyone."

Millie's lips pinched together as she sat down at the small round kitchen table. "I walked to the pharmacy yesterday, and I heard that the youngest Langford boy is back in town."

Small towns. Where everyone knows your business—often before you do.

"He was the rowdy one who went gallivanting all over the country to rodeos," Millie added. "I think you were sweet on him in high school."

"He was a friend, yes," Sara said carefully.

"Well. I hope he doesn't think he can come around and start that up again. You deserve a steady, hardworking fella. One with a *real* job."

"You don't need to worry. Like I said, I'm not interested in finding anyone. My focus is on the clinic, and I have plenty of company at the cabin to keep me occupied." Sara raised an eyebrow. "In fact, just last week someone dropped off the most beautiful cat. All white, except for a black tail. Purrs like an engine, declawed and fixed, and she's super friendly. She would be wonderful company for someone."

"No cats," Warren called out from his chair. "Got no use for a cat."

"No cats," Millie echoed softly, winding her fingers together on the table.

From her expression, Sara knew there was hope. "Well. I'll try to find her a good home. She's certainly an affectionate lap kitty." Sara finished combining the chili ingredients in the slow cooker and set the dial to High, then gave Warren and Millie their cups of coffee before tidying up. "If you think of any friends who might enjoy the company of a very sweet cat, let me know."

"Hhhmpf." Warren pointed the remote at the TV and turned on a 1960s Western.

"Have you given any more thought to those senior condos across town? They're a lot newer than this place, and each unit even has its own washer and dryer. How nice is that? You wouldn't have to walk down a long hall, then take stairs down to a dark and creepy basement. Where I'd bet there are huge *spiders*."

"Haven't seen more than a few." Millie set her jaw. "And we're fine right here."

"The condo place has a free shuttle van, so you'd never need to worry about keeping appointments if I can't help you that day." Sara kept unspooling the familiar litany, knowing it probably wouldn't do a bit of good. "And it's just a half block from the Senior Center. You could go there for a nice hot lunch every day and visit with people. It's important to get out and socialize."

Her gaze slid away. "This is all we need."

"But you can afford something nicer, Aunt Millie. Wouldn't you like a view of the Rockies instead of just a side street in town? More space? And instead of a tub, they even have walk-in showers—"

"We're fine, right here."

Sara knew from her aunt's stern expression that the conversation was over. Again.

Millie lowered her voice. "Now, young lady, we need to talk about that money you keep depositing in our account. I was just going over our bank statement this morning and found your deposit. You've done it twice now. It's unnecessary, and it needs to stop."

"But you could've sold the cabin, instead of keeping it for me. You could sure use that money now."

"As I recall, the mortgage payments on your clinic are pretty substantial." Millie gave her a shrewd look. "All well and good, but what if you run into trouble and can't make some payments? You could lose every penny you've put into that place. And then where would you be? Out on your ear. You need to put your extra money into your own savings, not ours. You need it more than a couple of old folks like us."

"But—"

"We want you to have that cabin—as our gift, because you're like the child we never had." Her eyes twinkled. "We'll get the paperwork figured one of these days, when our lawyer is back in town. Consider it an early inheritance."

Sara flinched at the cold reality of a time when they would no longer be here. "I don't even want to think of that day, Aunt Millie."

"Neither of us is in perfect health. When the good Lord wants us, we'll be ready," she said simply. "Whenever that is."

She'd tried to talk to them both a number of times since

she'd moved back to Pine Bend, and they'd still insisted on letting her have the cabin rent- and payment-free.

Thank goodness the two of them had looked to the future and given her their power of attorney, as well as adding her name to their accounts so she could help manage things if they grew incapable…and, coincidentally, so she could simply deposit her monthly cabin payments on her own. If she handed them checks, she doubted they'd ever cash them.

Yet she also knew just how slim their savings were.

"I would be making rent or mortgage payments to someone else, if you hadn't let me use the cabin. So I'm paying it off, just as any buyer would. But I do save money, so I'm not going to run into anything I can't handle."

"So you think," Millie retorted.

Sara belatedly remembered their medical bills, and how devastating debt had changed their lives. She wished she could call back her words.

"You're right." Sara glanced up at the clock on the wall and retrieved the coat she'd draped over the sofa as she headed for the door. "But you and Uncle Warren have always been like parents to me, and treating you right means a lot to me now. Case closed. Gotta run—see you both tomorrow!"

Millie's voice followed her into the hallway. "We will talk about this again. And don't forget to steer clear of that Langford boy. Apples don't fall far from the tree, and you know he'll only be trouble."

Millie had a ready cliché for almost every occasion, which usually made Sara smile fondly to herself. But today Millie's proclamation was delivered with a fierce note of worry impossible to miss.

How much had Millie known?

It had been a truly stupid, naive idea, hoping to jar her

self-absorbed parents' marriage out of its downward spiral by flirting with Tate. She'd never had a boyfriend, and she hadn't stopped to think that real feelings might develop and someone—both of them—could be hurt.

In the end, Tate had just shrugged and walked away as if they'd been nothing more that casual friends. But had Millie seen how much Sara had come to love him? How heartbroken she'd been when it was all over?

Millie had never heard the whole story, though, and probably figured it was just another example of a Langford callously hurting someone she loved. Given her outspoken nature, Sara didn't even want to think about what the elderly woman might say—or do—if she came face-to-face with Tate now.

Sara climbed behind the wheel of her truck and rested her forehead on the steering wheel with a long sigh.

Proud, independent, hardworking ranch folks didn't just fade to meek and compliant because they got old. It might take an earthquake to get them to move to a place better suited to their growing disabilities. Millie might never stop fussing about the payments Sara was depositing into their money market account.

But now she had another worry.

As Millie and Warren aged, they were becoming more outspoken—with little filtering of what they said. *Please, please don't say anything to Tate.*

It would be embarrassing. Awkward.

And completely without merit, because she certainly didn't harbor a single thought about starting a relationship with him or anyone else.

She would make her clinic a success. And then, on her little piece of the Montana foothills that held such a connection to her beloved aunt and uncle, she would happily live out her dreams alone.

Alone.

It had all been perfectly clear until this moment…so why did those dreams suddenly ring hollow?

Saturday dawned clear and bright, perfect for a second ride up into the north pasture to finish riding the fence. It only made sense to start where he'd left off last time—near Sara's cabin—so he wouldn't miss a section. He wasn't *really* expecting to run into her again.

Yet as he passed the one point where the cabin would partially come into view, he found himself pulling Blondie to a halt and peering through the trees.

No dogs barked this time. The place looked quiet. After a few minutes he urged the mare on, following the fence line as it wound up through the trees, across a meadow and into a heavy stand of pines.

The terrain became more difficult after this, he recalled, as it rose to a higher elevation, the property line skimming the edge of an area with rocky outcroppings and massive boulders. Several mountain streams would tumble down through the rocks come the spring thaw, and Silver Bells Falls would roar over a sharp cliff almost a hundred feet high.

He twisted in the saddle and withdrew his Canon SLR camera, attached a 100-300mm lens and rode on. From the fence line, maybe a hundred yards ahead, he would be able to see the falls for the first time during the winter.

Would it be a glittering ice sculpture, its water flow frozen in time? Nothing but bare rock until the spring thaw? His anticipation grew as he guided Blondie toward the last bend.

Almost there.

Blondie suddenly snorted. Reared high. Then lurched to the right and took off bucking, barely missing the shoulder-high boulders in her path that left little room for maneuvering her into a tight circle, then a halt.

When he got her stopped and facing back toward the falls she blew noisily, her sides heaving and her head raised high, her total focus on whatever lay beyond that last bend.

Bears were still in hibernation up here.

A wolf? Coyote?

He reached for the stock of the rifle in his scabbard and considered a warning shot. But hesitated, knowing that Blondie would likely go crazy at the sound.

At the rustle of branches up the trail, her head jerked even higher and bobbed up and down. Her muscles bunched until she felt like a coiled spring, though this time his camera was back in the saddlebag and he was better prepared. "Easy girl…easy…"

Whistling. Was that someone *whistling*?

A small form appeared on the path, bundled up in a puffy red jacket and oversize hood that gave him—or her—the appearance of someone in an astronaut's suit, one hand gripping what appeared to be a can of bear spray.

The person stopped and stared. "*Tate?* What are you doing up here?"

Blondie snorted. Fidgeted. Tate urged her forward, until he and Sara were just a few yards apart. "I could ask the same thing."

She gave him an incredulous look. "You care if someone hikes on Langford land—way out here? How many thousands of acres do you people own, anyway?"

"Of course I don't care about hikers—as long as they don't damage any fencing. Poachers, yes." His gaze fell on the bold white letters printed on a black strap slung messenger-style across the front of her jacket. Nikon.

"I was taking pictures," she said defensively. "Ever

since I moved back, I've been dying to get up here again. It's been years and years."

"The high school senior picnic?"

"Not since then. I hardly ever came home once I left for college." She angled a reproachful look at him. "You scared me half to death when I heard you coming. I was afraid you might be a wolf."

He chuckled. "Hence the bear spray?"

"I thought I should bring *something*, and it was all I had. I don't own any weapons."

Impatient at standing still, Blondie started tossing her head and dancing sideways. Tate settled her with a hand on her neck. "I'm beginning to think this mare will never make a steady, bombproof trail horse."

"With enough years and miles, maybe." Sara stepped to one side to allow him to pass. "Well…um…I should let you get back to work. I suppose you're checking the rest of the fence line?"

"That, and I was hoping to get some shots of the falls. I've never been back here during the winter."

Her eyes widened in surprise. "You're into photography too?"

"Since I took a class in college. I'm just an amateur, really. But with digital, I can take a hundred shots to get the one I like. And I like manipulating the results on the computer."

She grinned up at him. "Me too. Do you remember the days when our parents' generation used film and had it developed at the drug store? Every shot was expensive, so they didn't waste a single one."

"And most of the photos were pretty bad. I would offer you a ride back to your place, but I'm guessing Blondie isn't quite ready for extra passengers."

"I'm just happy to be hiking on a day like this, but

thanks." Sara hitched a thumb over her shoulder. "The falls aren't far—just around that next bend. I'll follow and hold your horse so you can climb high up onto the rocks for the best view."

He'd expected that he'd only be able to take some photographs from the saddle, because he'd left the halter back at the barn today and tying an agitated, green mare with slender leather reins could spell trouble—and a long walk home. "I'd really appreciate that, if you don't mind."

"If you go just a little higher, there's a great lookout point at the top of the hill. You can see part of my cabin roof through the pine trees, and if you look to the south you can see my aunt and uncle's—er, your ranch buildings. Be sure to go up. It's only another five minutes or so."

He dismounted and followed Sara up the hill, then retrieved his camera from his saddlebag and handed her the reins. "I won't be but a minute."

"No worries. Just take your time, because it's really beautiful up there. I've got Solitaire on my phone, and Blondie and I can have a chat about good trail manners while you're gone."

"Thanks, Sara." Without thinking, he gave her a quick one-armed hug of appreciation, just as he might have years ago. It felt so right—so *normal* that he might have even held her a little longer, then brushed a casual kiss against her cheek and not have given it a second thought.

For just a split second it seemed as if she was melting into his embrace. But then she stiffened, took a step back and busied herself with checking the cinch on his saddle.

"Go on now, have a good time," she said briskly as she tightened it a notch. "Turn left when you see a single, spindly birch. We'll be here waiting."

Well. That was awkward.

He nodded and turned to brace a hand on a post and vault over the fence, then jogged through a maze of boulders and scrub brush to the rough, rocky terrain that rose far above him, far as he could see.

No trees.

The ascent grew steeper. Wishing he'd worn climbing boots instead of his Tony Lamas, he climbed farther, his leather soles slipping on the weathered rocks.

He rounded a jagged shelf of rock, and suddenly he was nose-to-bark with a slender, anemic-looking birch that against all odds had taken root in a tiny patch of dirt. "Now, that's an example of determination," he muttered.

He took a few steps back and photographed it from several angles, catching its stark bleached-bone trunk against the rough granite where deep crevices still held a dusting of snow.

He turned left and continued on to a narrow ledge. And there it was—frozen in time by the harsh winter.

The top of the falls was still another fifty feet up, but from here he could see the entire cascade of water, turned to fantastical shapes by wind and cold, alternating with the occasional warm days of a typical Montana winter that allowed more water to fall.

With the sunlight glinting through the ice it appeared to be a waterfall made of a massive flow of diamonds.

Moving back and forth on the ledge, he photographed the waterfall from every angle, nudging the settings on the camera in minute increments. If he came back a thousand times, he suspected it would be different every time, with the variations in the angle and intensity of sunlight and shadow.

He glanced at the time on his cell phone, then turned away with regret. He'd been up here forty-five minutes already. He shouldn't have been gone so long, leaving Sara holding his horse.

Yet on his way back—when he reached the birch tree, her words came back to him and he resolutely turned upward toward the overlook she'd mentioned. Five more minutes, she'd said. Not far.

His jaw dropped when he reached a small plateau at the top of the hill. The Big Sky Montana slogan barely did the view justice. To the west, the jagged, sawtooth peaks of the Rockies marched along the horizon, towering over him and seeming close enough to touch. The vast, brilliant blue sky stretched in every direction, like an endless, perfect bowl of robin's-egg blue.

There were the Branson ranch buildings far below to the south—tiny as miniature toys. He shifted his gaze to the east, to the forest he'd just ridden through, then beyond the meadow, to find Sara's cabin roof.

Strange. It had to be there…though maybe the dark green steel was camouflaged by the surrounding pines.

He leaned forward, squinting at the terrain…then realized why he couldn't see it. Was that a haze drifting above the spot where the cabin should be?

Now thin plumes of smoke shot skyward, darkened, and in the space of a few seconds began billowing above the trees.

The cabin was on fire.

Chapter Five

Sara leaned against Blondie's warm winter coat and bit her lower lip as she stared at her cell phone and strategized her next move. "Solitaire is definitely not my thing," she said glumly. "You'd be better at it than me, and you're a *horse.*"

The mare turned her head to look at her and gave her a little nudge, then her shoulder muscles stiffened beneath Sara's jacket and she abruptly raised her head toward the hill, her ears pricked.

Sara sighed. *Not again.*

Over the space of the past hour the silly mare had shied at chipmunks. Startled when a hawk flew overhead. Then there'd been a slight rustle of branches that could have been—well, anyone's guess—but that had sent Blondie flying backward, nearly jerking the reins out of Sara's hands.

Now she was bobbing her head, as if trying to focus on something, which probably meant there was going to be yet *another* ruckus. Sara stroked the mare's golden neck. "Easy, girl. There's nothing—"

"Sara," Tate called from somewhere up on the hill. He sounded breathless. "Quick—call 911."

Startled, she spun around. She could see him now, winding through the massive boulders strewn midway down the steep slope. "What—why?"

"Fire—at your place. I saw smoke."

A sick sensation clenched her stomach as she jammed a fingertip at the numbers on her keypad—then noticed the screen showed just one bar...and the call didn't go through.

All of those defenseless animals—trapped. No way out. *Oh, Lord—please help us save them.*

A few seconds later Tate vaulted over the fence, slowing down as he approached the mare. He jerked his phone up to his face. "I still don't have any reception. You?"

"No." As soon as Tate grabbed the reins from her, Sara took off running toward home. How far was it—a mile, maybe two? Her heartbeat thundered in her ears. The cabin was *impossibly* far...

Hoofbeats thundered up behind her and she looked over her shoulder as Tate pulled to a stop. He reached down for her. "You can run, but this would be faster. Are you game? If she starts to tense you can slip off." He slid his left foot out of the stirrup.

Sara debated for just a heartbeat, then used the stirrup and his hand to land lightly behind the cantle of the saddle. "Please, Lord—let this work. Please, Lord—"

Blondie shied to one side, her back bowed like a coiled spring, ready to explode into a bucking spree— but Tate distracted her by reining her into a tight circle, then pointed her nose toward home and pushed her into a lope—then faster.

As if she knew she was heading in the direction of her barn, she opened up and flew through the timber, Tate guiding her around boulders and trees. In the meadow she picked up more speed yet.

He settled her into a slower lope long enough to check the bars on his cell phone and hand the phone to Sara. "Got three bars here—make the call."

She made the 911 call and disconnected, then continued to pray. If the cabin was already engulfed, there would be no chance of saving it or the animals inside. But even if it was still small, what chance was there?

The volunteer firemen in Pine Bend had to leave their jobs and ranches; some to the station for the fire trucks, others straight to the fire. But it was nearly a fifty-minute drive for her to reach town, and with the curvy road leading from the highway up to the cabin, they probably couldn't make it any faster.

Tate slowed as they neared the cabin, and Sara slid off before he'd even stopped. She raced for the fence. Even from here she could smell the heavy stench of burning rubber, and the smoke made it hard to breathe.

"Wait—let me go," Tate shouted. "I can lift the heavier cages—where are the extinguishers?"

She looked back. Tate was already on the ground, leading Blondie toward her at a trot. The mare exhaled with a gusty sigh, her thick winter coat damp with sweat. Steam rolled off her neck and sides into the chilly air.

"I—I—" Sara wavered, frustration flooding through her. The mare was breathing too hard to tie up and leave. "I need to go. I know where everything is. Come when you can."

Charging through the underbrush, she sped past the shed and little barn, then skidded to a stop. Black smoke was billowing from underneath the garage door, nearly obliterating the view of the structure. Something inside exploded with the force of a bomb, then again—aerosol cans, probably.

Rushing up onto the deck, she felt the door for heat,

then cautiously opened it and felt the five rescue cats rush past her ankles to freedom.

Smoke poured from underneath the door leading out to the garage but—so far—she could see no flames inside the cabin itself.

It would only be a matter of time.

Coughing, she hurriedly packed kitchen towels against the base of the door, then ran to the dog cages, leashing and taking the six dogs outside by threes and tying them on the other side of the truck, then she went after Theodore's bulky cage—which she dragged to the front door.

Theodore was nowhere to be seen.

"Theodore! Pretty bird—pretty bird!" She spun on her heel, searching the rafters. The loft railing.

Tate appeared behind her, his form hazy. "What's left?"

She coughed. "What about Blondie?"

"This is more important—*you're* more important."

"Theodore—can you see him?" she called over her shoulder as she raced up the loft stairs to the bird's favorite haunt, while Tate searched below.

The smoke inside the cabin was rising, pooling in the open rafters. In the loft it was hard to see and even harder to breathe. If the bird hadn't headed for the lower level it might already be—

"Found him!" Tate shouted. "But he isn't looking too perky."

"Don't touch him—just try to corral him." She took the steps three at a time and found Tate crouching in a corner of the great room, behind an upholstered love seat. "He could bite off your fingers."

The bird was crouched in the corner, his wings held away from his body, his breathing labored. He swayed on his feet as she drew closer.

Grabbing a fleecy afghan from the back of the love

seat she gently wrapped him, his head covered, and took him to his cage.

"I'll take that. Where do you want him?"

"Over in the shed by the corral. He'll be out of the breeze, and away from the cats and dogs. It's less smoky over there."

"Got it." He took off with the bird and she spun on her heel, mentally ticking a list of the animals that were inside, then she ran for the fire extinguishers and set them by the front door.

Building codes required a fire wall between a garage and dwelling—had that been honored here? How long would it hold? Had there even been any inspections during the do-it-yourself project Uncle Warren had undertaken?

The steel roof seemed to be fending off random sparks, but losing the cabin itself was only a matter of time. The wisps of smoke coming through the seams of the pine paneling proved it.

Grabbing a laundry basket, she hurriedly threw in her laptop, bag of camera gear and important file folders from a drawer in her desk, then scooped up irreplaceable mementos—photo albums, keepsakes—and ran outside to put them in her truck, which she'd not pulled into the garage, thank goodness.

She turned to go back, still trying to draw fresh air into her smoke-filled lungs.

Tate met her halfway and gently grabbed her arms. "Don't."

She struggled to free herself. "But I need to. Everything I own is—"

"It's not worth it. Look."

The garage door buckled from the intense heat within, releasing a wall of flames that licked at the exterior siding and edged toward the cabin.

More explosions.

Then another that shook the ground and sent a blast of heat sweeping over her that felt like liquid fire. "Oh, my Lord—I'll bet that was a gas can."

"There's nothing more you can do, Sara. It's over."

"But I've got the fire extinguishers. I've got to protect the cabin."

"You wouldn't stand a chance, honey. It isn't worth your life."

Defeated, she turned limp and dropped her head against his chest. He wrapped his arms around her and held her close, suffusing her with his warmth and strength.

He stilled. *"Listen."*

The faint sound of sirens filtered through the trees, coming closer. But slowly. Not nearly fast enough—and that thought gripped her heart like an iron fist.

She'd wanted paperwork on the cabin. A mortgage, or contract for deed, or *something*. But while Sara had gently wrangled with Warren and Millie, they'd only brushed aside her concerns and refused to discuss it. No one had brought up one important fact.

They were older now, and more forgetful. The cabin had been sitting empty over a year. *What if it wasn't insured?*

Gene Carlson pulled off his volunteer-fire-chief's helmet and swiped at his forehead with the sleeve of his heavy turnout coat as he studied the front of the garage. The other three volunteers were gathering their gear and rolling up the hoses.

"You were sure fortunate," he muttered. "This old cabin was remodeled, right?"

She nodded. "By my uncle."

"Most of these really remote places were built generations ago and don't even come close to code. But he did add a fire wall between the house and garage."

"Apparently he did a good job. Right?"

"Actually, far better than the building codes require. That wall and the steel roof made all the difference."

"I can't thank you and your crew enough for coming all the way up here." Her arms wrapped around her middle, Sara gave him a wan smile, her face pale and smudged with smoke.

She looked so worn-out that Tate wanted to pull her into his arms just to keep her steady. He settled for draping an arm around her shoulders and drawing her close to his side. "Can you tell what started the fire?"

"I need to look it over again before I write up my report." Gene settled his helmet back on his head. "The heaviest charring is around the electrical control panel in the garage, so I believe that was the point of origin. My guess is that mice chewed the insulation on some wires. Didn't you say that the place was empty for quite a while?"

Sara nodded. "I moved in the first of February."

"I'd have an electrician take a look at all of the wiring in the cabin, just to be safe. Next time you might not fare as well. As it is, you aren't going to be able to stay here for a while. Even with large exhaust fans it'll take a long time to air out. Your insurance agent can get you set up with those."

Sara heaved a sigh, hoping there *was* an insurance agent to ask. "I'll check on that."

The charred garage door now lay in a twisted heap to one side, the black maw of the double garage still emitting faint plumes of smoke.

The stench of wet cinders and burning rubber still filled the air.

Tate tipped his head toward the other volunteers. "Can I help?"

A grin creased the man's weathered cheeks. "You'll have enough to do after we're gone. But if you really feel like helping, we can always use more volunteers. Only had four of us today—the others were out of town or just couldn't get away."

"I would if I could, but I'll be moving on in a few months. Sorry."

Gene studied him for a long moment, his brow furrowed. "Aren't you one of the Langford boys? You might've gone to school with one of my sons—Jared Carlson."

"Smartest kid in his graduating class. A year ahead of me, I think. Quarterback, his senior year."

"He's a college grad, headed for the big city—then he decided he'd rather be ranching than fighting rush-hour traffic." The man beamed with obvious pride. "Real glad to have him back, and he's even happier. You might want to think twice about leaving God's country behind."

Gene glanced over at the volunteer firemen, who were waiting by the tanker fire truck. "Well, folks, we'll be on our way. I'll stop by sometime tomorrow to sift through the debris and see if I can find a more definitive cause for the fire."

Sara reached out to shake his hand. "I appreciate everything, Mr. Carlson."

As soon as the fire crew left, Sara stepped away from Tate's embrace and rubbed her upper arms. "It's only midafternoon and it's already getting colder out. I need to get the animals moved, and I imagine you need to start for home. You have a long ride ahead of you."

The cats had lurked at the edge of the timber. After she caught all five and put them into small carriers, she loaded them into the front of the truck. The three smallest dogs she put in the backseat.

"Are you going to have enough space for all of those animals at the clinic?"

"I have no choice now. The cabin smells smoky, and that's bad for all of them—especially the parrot." She eyed the three bigger dogs she'd tied to separate trees by the truck. "But I'll pick up exhaust fans tomorrow and start cleaning. Maybe in a couple days they can come back here."

Tate frowned. "Surely you aren't going to stay here tonight."

She shrugged. "The electrical panel in the cabin is still fine. I've got lights and the furnace works. After I take the animals into town I can get started washing curtains and scrubbing the smokiness from the walls."

"Here's a different thought—take the animals to my place. I've got empty box stalls for the dogs, and a warm tack room for the cats. As for the bird—its cage could go in there too. It's far closer than hauling them all to town—and either way it'll take two trips."

She hesitated. "That seems like a lot of bother for you."

"None at all. I'm glad to help an old friend. I don't have any extra furnished bedrooms, but I know Jess and his wife have some spare guest rooms."

"That isn't necessary. Really."

"It is. At least for tonight. If that smoky air in the cabin isn't safe for the animals, it sure won't do you any good." Tate looked at the time on his phone. "I'll tell you what—I'll head for home with Blondie now so I can get her back before dark. You go ahead and settle in your animals however you see fit. You know the barn better than I do. I'll probably get there by the time you finish your second trip."

"I feel really bad, making extra work for you, though."

"It's nothing."

"But—"

He gave a firm shake of his head. "I'll let Jess and Abby know you'll be coming for a night or so. Everything in your cabin is probably too smoky to wear, so bring any clothes you'd like to wash. Tomorrow afternoon I'll be over here to help with the cleanup. Okay?"

"No. You've got a lot to do as it is. I'll take care of it."

"Neighbors help each other around here, Sara. And believe me, if you don't let me pitch in, I will *never* hear the end of it from my grandma."

She stared at the blackened garage for a long moment, her eyes weary and a little dazed. "You're a good man, Tate. I'd forgotten just how kind you are."

She rested her hands on his shoulders and rose on her tiptoes to kiss him lightly on the cheek. And then she hurried to her truck without a backward glance.

He stared after her, the world shifting beneath his feet.

Since she'd come back to town, nothing had been said. No parameters had been discussed. But he'd understood their tacit agreement—whatever they'd had between them was in the past, and they were practically strangers now.

So why did that swift, innocent kiss of gratitude send a shock wave clear to his core, and suddenly seem to mean so much more?

"You poor, poor girl," Tate's grandma Betty tutted when he and Sara walked into the kitchen at the Langford Ranch late that evening. "I'm so glad Tate told us about your dilemma. You are certainly welcome to stay with us as long as you like. Right, Abby?"

Abby moved forward with a warm smile and gave Sara a hug. "Absolutely."

Embarrassed, Sara tried to dredge up an answering

smile, but knew it probably ended up more of a grimace. "Sorry—I imagine I still smell smoky."

Abby waved away her concerns. "And who wouldn't? Sounds like you've had a terrible day."

"But eat first, while everything is nice and hot. You can get cleaned up later." Betty bustled over to the oven and pulled out a pan of rolls, then lifted the lid of a Crock-Pot and stirred the contents. "We've got a hearty beef stew, parmesan rolls with whipped herb butter, and blueberry pie."

"It all sounds wonderful." Sara breathed in the rich, delicious aromas. "I never imagined the day ending like this. Thank you."

"The powder room is just around the corner if you need it." Betty's silver hair shone under the kitchen lights as she brought the rolls and butter to the oblong oak kitchen table. "Otherwise, just have a seat. You must be exhausted."

The table was already set, with emerald place mats and white dishes, and Abby was bringing the black crockery liner of the slow cooker to the table when Sara came back from washing her hands.

"Just sit anywhere. The twins ate earlier and have gone to bed, and Jess is back out in the barn waiting for a mare that should be foaling any minute." Abby smiled. "I'm afraid this will be a very informal meal, and that you've only got the two of us for company."

Sara sank into a chair. The warmth of the cheery kitchen made her suddenly feel incredibly tired. "I am so grateful to you both."

"Let's pray," Betty murmured from across the table. "Thank you, Lord, for bringing Sara here tonight. For saving her cabin, and for keeping her and the animals safe. Bless all those who will be helping her life return to normalcy during the next weeks, and please protect Abby during her journey to California. Finally, bless the food we are about to eat. Amen."

"Leaving wintry Montana for sunshine sounds rather nice," Sara murmured. "Will you be gone long?"

"Two weeks. I'm in a distance-learning PhD program, but three times of year I need to be on-campus for seminars and consultation with my advisers. I started last September."

Fascinated, Sara cocked her head. "That's impressive. What's your major?"

"Special Ed, with my focus on autism research."

"It's a fancy university," Betty added with a mischievous twinkle in her eyes. "Abby isn't one to ever boast, but I was snoopy and looked it up on my computer. It's one of the top ten programs in the whole country and admission is highly competitive. We're very proud of our Abby. And Chloe too. She has a master's in…was it in publishing? No—creative writing. She even sent a young adult novel off to a publisher last summer."

"*And* she submitted a cookbook to a different publisher," Abby added. "She hasn't heard anything yet, but we're sure she'll succeed. She's a wonderful writer."

"Goodness. I'm impressed."

"During spring semester she's been teaching at a college near Butte, so we just see her on weekends now and then," Abby said as she ladled bowls of stew and handed them around the table, then passed the herb butter and basket of rolls. "Tate tells me that you had a lot of rescue animals in your cabin, but they're all at his place now."

"I'm grateful that he suggested it. Otherwise I would've had two long trips into town tonight, and there isn't really enough space at the clinic anyhow."

"Very handy, indeed." Betty glanced between Tate and Sara, a gleam of curiosity in her eyes and a faint smile playing on her lips. "I believe I remember you from years ago, dear. Weren't you and Tate friends, senior year?"

Sara knew a matchmaker when she saw one, and could already imagine the wheels turning in Betty's head. "*Friends.* I remember him being a really nice kid back then."

Betty smiled at Tate and chuckled. "I know some folks said you could be a bit rambunctious at times. But you were always just the sweetest, most affectionate little boy."

The back door closed with a soft click and Sara looked over her shoulder.

Jess had come inside. He flipped his Stetson onto a hook and hung up his jacket, then shucked off his boots. "Yes he was," he drawled, a teasing glint in his eyes. "Our little Tater was absolutely the sweetest *ever*...and he still is. Right, Grandma?"

"*Boys.* Enough. Jess, you be quiet and go wash up so you can have some blueberry pie." Abby rolled her eyes. "They're all grown men, but when the brothers are in the same room it's like a pack of fifth graders. Don't pay any attention."

"That's because Jess and Devlin never really grew up," Tate said solemnly. "It's a constant trial for us all."

Jess came back into the kitchen and poured himself a cup of coffee, offered everyone else some, then took a chair at the end of the table. "We've got a brand-new paint filly. Pretty little head and the wildest markings I've seen. Ten down and five more mares to go."

"The girls will be thrilled." Abby exchanged weary glances with Betty. "We had quite a time getting them to sleep this evening. They've missed all of the other foals and didn't want to miss this one too."

"But you never know how long things will take. The mare could've waited to foal until the middle of the night."

Betty headed for the coffeepot and offered refills, then eyed the table. "Is everyone ready for pie?"

Sara jumped to her feet and helped deliver the dessert plates to the table as Betty cut each slice and topped it with a scoop of vanilla ice cream, while Abby cleared the table.

"This pie is amazing," Sara exclaimed after her first bite. "I am in awe."

"So am I." Abby gave Betty an affectionate pat on the arm. "I have watched her over and over and have taken copious notes, but my pies still don't come close. It has to be a gift."

Sara had come into this home feeling stressed and worn-out, only thinking about a hot shower and a soft bed. But now she glanced around at everyone at the table and absorbed the sense of family—the obvious camaraderie, the love, the gentle teasing. A sense of wistfulness washed through her. This was what she had always dreamed of as a child.

From the time she'd been old enough to be at home alone she *had* been—while her parents worked long hours and volunteered their spare time to good causes, barely landing at home to bicker and sleep before starting the next day of commitments to career and community.

Sara had resented her loneliness: all of the times she'd had no parent in the crowd at a school event or someone to talk to at home. She'd felt guilty over selfishly begrudging her parents the time they'd spent on people and causes more important to them than any sense of family life.

There'd been no sweet grandma like Betty at home to take up the slack…no siblings to fill the void. Just the sorry example of what marriage was like, which had dogged her ever since and kept her from ever risking that same mistake. So why on earth had she kissed Tate?

Simple gratitude. That had to be it.

He'd given her a feeling of warmth and security, when
he'd kept his arm around her shoulders after the fire.
Something she'd rarely felt. Surely just the kindness of a
friend and nothing more.

Though, from the startled look on his face, her kiss
hadn't exactly been a welcome gesture. Her cheeks burning, she'd quickly turned away and hadn't looked back.

She shoved aside her maudlin thoughts and found Betty
watching her with concern in her faded blue eyes.

"We shouldn't be chattering away and keeping you
up—you must be nearly dead on your feet." Betty stood
and put her dishes in the sink. "Come with me, and we'll
get you settled. Did you have any clothing I can wash and
dry for you?"

"I…um…did bring a small bag, but you don't need to
do that for me." She went to fetch the small plastic bag
she'd dropped by the front door. "Just point me to the
laundry room."

"Goodness, no." Betty held out her hand until Sara re-
luctantly gave it to her. "I'll do that while you are getting
ready for bed."

"I'll check on all of your animals when I get home,"
Tate called out. "Any instructions?"

She paused at the kitchen door and turned. "I brought
their food and put it in the tack room. I'll be over first
thing in the morning to take care of them. Thanks, Tate,
for everything."

Betty led her to a bedroom at the end of the hall with
a flower-sprigged wallpaper, lacy curtains and a pretty
pastel quilt on the bed.

"Abby and I just made up the bed with clean sheets, and
that stack of towels on the dresser is for you. We thought
you might be more comfortable in here since it has its own
bathroom and shower."

"It's lovely. Thank you so much."

Betty tsked under her breath as she turned back a corner of the quilt and top sheet and fluffed the pillows. "Now you try to sleep as late as you can. I'm sure Tate can figure out the feeding of whatever you've stowed at his place, so don't worry about that. Promise? If we've all gone to church by the time you're up, I'll have a nice breakfast laid out for you when you get up."

Between the sweetly feminine room, a hovering, solicitous grandma, the family's kindness and all that had happened today, Sara felt her eyes start to burn. "I—I can't thank you enough, Betty."

"Everything will be all right, dear. When I start to worry, I remember my favorite Bible verse in Philippians, and just give it over to God. 'In every thing by prayer and supplication with thanksgiving let your requests be made known unto God. And the peace of God, which passeth all understanding, shall keep your hearts and minds through Christ Jesus.' That one always feels so reassuring."

As if she sensed Sara's brimming emotions, Betty gave her a warm hug and patted her back. There was a twinkle in her eyes when she stepped away. "Maybe this was all part of God's plan for you—coming back when you did. Maybe you'll discover a more wonderful future than you ever expected. Sleep well."

Long after she'd taken a long, hot shower, Sara snuggled under the covers, but sleep eluded her as worries endlessly circled through her thoughts like moths orbiting a security light, worries that had plagued her for some time and now loomed even larger after the fire.

The long-term owner of her clinic had been a curmudgeon, from all the accounts she'd heard, so the clinic hadn't been as busy and profitable as it could've been.

That, followed by two new owners in less than a year, wasn't exactly a confidence builder for clients.

She *had* to build the clientele, and soon.

The clinic mortgage payments had to be paid monthly, absolutely on time. She'd be paying off her vet-school loans until she was old and gray. Just as important, she would be making regular house payments to Warren and Millie.

Every. Single. Month.

But now there was her other worry—insurance on the cabin. Millie and Warren went to bed promptly at nine, and there was no point awakening them—especially if the call would upset them. It would be far better to see them in person before they heard the news from someone else.

If there was no insurance, she would pay for all of the repairs herself…because she knew full well that they didn't have the money.

But when she finally started to drift off to sleep, it wasn't the clinic, the fire or her monumental debts that were swimming through her thoughts. It was the twinkle in Betty's eyes before she'd wished Sara good-night, coupled with the moment Sara had impulsively kissed Tate…

And the crazy wish that someday, he would kiss her back.

Chapter Six

Tate's grandma Betty hadn't been kidding about breakfast.

Caramel rolls. Homemade cinnamon-streusel bread. A fruit platter. And she'd also left a sweet note thanking Sara for coming, asking for her cell phone number and directing her to the breakfast casserole in the fridge, with directions for reheating portions in the microwave or stove.

Sara had heard the family's SUV pulling out just as she was getting dressed and felt a stab of regret, knowing she should have gone to church, as well. But she'd awakened too late. And though Betty had washed her clothes and left them neatly folded by her bedroom door, none of them were respectful enough for church—just old jeans and faded T-shirts, coupled with the smoky, battered hiking boots she'd worn when she'd come last night.

All of her animals were probably complaining about the breakfast delay and driving Tate crazy by now, though. She needed to get over there and take care of them, visit Warren and Millie and start cleaning up smoke damage at the cabin. And after the volunteer fire chief investigated the fire origin, the garage, as well.

A busy day.

She rubbed her forehead with her fingertips, hoping to

quiet the headache starting to build, then poured hot coffee into the travel mug Betty had left for her, ate quickly and went back to strip the linens in her room.

Forty minutes later she pulled up at the barns at Warren and Millie's ranch—now just another division of the Langford ranch, she reminded herself.

From within the horse barn she heard the sound of dogs barking and the muffled sound of the parrot rapping out one of the *Hamilton* songs…probably the fourth one on the album, so he had a ways to go in his repertoire.

The racket increased when she stepped inside the barn, where she found Tate brushing a fidgety bay gelding cross-tied in the aisle. Tate glanced at her and nodded hello, then led the horse down the aisle to a box stall.

As soon as she spoke, the dogs started yelping and jumping against the front of the two box stalls she'd commandeered for them yesterday. The cats began yowling in the tack room.

And now Theodore began yelling his usual refrain when he thought it was time to eat. *"Emergency! Emergency! Ringadingding!"* in a voice loud enough to wake the dead.

Where on earth had he learned that—from a cartoon show?

"Really sorry about the noise," she called out. "I promise I'll have all of the animals gone by tomorrow for sure. Maybe even tonight."

Tate didn't answer and she thought he might be frustrated and angry.

But when he turned to walk back up the aisle with a young paint, she could see he was laughing and she felt a funny little rush of awareness wash through her.

"I'll have to say that this has been an experience," he

drawled. "If you deal with this noise all the time, I think you deserve a medal."

"No—the animals were settled at the cabin. Once I get them all fed they should be better. Has it been…um… really difficult while handling the horses?"

He cross-tied the mare and began brushing her. "It's been fine, actually. Every new experience—every different sort of ruckus to tolerate—is good exposure. I usually have a radio station on loud for the same reason, but your friends have been more than enough."

She turned and went into the tack room to feed her cats and Theodore. Four of the cats fled past her boots before she could stop them and disappeared into the hay stall. Only one came for her *kittykittykitty* dinner call—the pure white female.

"Sorry," she muttered as she came out with stacked pans of dry dog food. "A few cats got away from me."

"That's a relief. *Three* got away when I carried a saddle out into the aisle. I was feeling pretty guilty." She thought she saw a twinkle in his eyes. "So at least it's not only me."

"It'll probably just be easier to let them be loose in the barn, from now on. I promise I'll get the rescues all caught when I take my animals home." She put three pans of kibble for large dogs in one stall, and three pans of kibble for smaller dogs in the other, then filled both water pails. "Thanks again for all of your help yesterday."

He rested a heavy saddle pad on the paint's back, then settled the saddle into place so gently that it might not have weighed more than a feather. The mare's ears swiveled, but she didn't flinch. "I didn't do that much. But you're welcome, anytime."

"And thanks for setting me up with a night at Jess and Abby's place. You were right—it would have been smoky and miserable back at the cabin."

He looked up from cinching the saddle. "So what do you think of my grandma?"

She leaned against the front of a stall. "She seemed familiar, so I must have seen her a time or two at school events. She's such a sweetheart."

"That she is." His lips twitched. "She also fancies herself as the family matchmaker, so consider yourself forewarned. After you went to bed she must have spent ten minutes at the table, extolling your virtues."

Since Jess and Devlin were taken, that left Tate…and *that* knowledge did something funny to her insides.

"I doubt it would take that long to list my better qualities," Sara said dryly. "She must have made some up."

"We all thought she made a good case. Especially when Grandma waggled her finger under my nose and said you were way too good for me. Jess really liked that part."

Sara guessed his crafty grandma was trying to entice him with forbidden fruit. "She does know you're leaving in a few months, right?"

"Sure does." He bridled the mare, then looked at Sara and grinned. "But when Grandma comes up with an idea, such barriers don't always matter. Therefore, I'm apologizing in advance for anything she says or does that might be…awkward."

Sara suppressed a smile. "Like saying that I've arrived at the *perfect* time—assuming that's because you're home now—or that I might have a more wonderful future than I ever could have guessed? From that mischievous sparkle in her eyes, I think she's already counting on wedding bells. Just so you know."

Tate groaned. "Sorry. Like I said—"

"No worries. I just need to let her know that I'm totally wrapped up in my career and have no plans to ever settle down." Sara rolled her eyes. "Even if I wanted to, I'd be an awful choice thanks to my awe-inspiring mountain of debt. Which, sadly, probably just got a whole lot worse."

"Because of the fire?"

Sara glanced at the big white clock on the wall and nodded. "I just hope Warren and Betty have insurance. They handle all that, and I guess I assumed it would be rolled in with their other policies—life and auto. They should be home from church by the time I get there, and believe me, I'll be doing some praying along the way."

She did exactly that on her way into town, then found herself hesitating to knock on their door. What if Warren became upset and had another stroke? Or Millie burst into tears over the home she'd loved so much?

Sara took a deep breath and knocked lightly, then a little louder. "Are you home?"

She heard the shuffling of feet across the wood floor, then the door opened wide. Warren stood before her in his dress slacks and a button-down plaid shirt.

"Well," he said gruffly. "Didn't expect to see you today."

Millie hovered at his elbow. "What a wonderful surprise, dear. The Weavers just dropped us off after church. Can you stay for lunch?"

"Um…no. I just wanted to share some news with you. In person."

Warren waved her in toward the sofa and closed the door, then slowly headed for his recliner. "I don't suppose this would be about the fire."

She felt her mouth drop open. "You heard?"

Millie nodded. "The entire volunteer fire department attends Pine Bend Community Church, so there was a lot of talk. Something like that is big news in a small town."

"We heard that you and your pets were safe, so that was

a relief," Warren added. "What we haven't heard about was the cause. Or the degree of damage."

"Gene—the fire chief—is going back today so he can take a longer look. Last night he guessed a bare wire might've sparked in the garage wall, behind the electrical panel. He said mice might've chewed on the wire insulation." She took a deep breath. "The cabin filled with smoke, but wasn't touched by the fire. I'll scrub the walls and floors, and run fans to try to clear out the smell."

"And the garage? I had a lot of tools and equipment in there."

"I haven't been inside, but the interior looks pretty well charred. I couldn't guess at the dollar amount. Which is why…" She said another brief, silent prayer. "The insurance adjuster needs to come out. Would you have his name and your policy number?"

Millie and Warren exchanged glances, then Millie worried at her lower lip. "I…don't know, dear. We've been away from there for so long."

Sara's heart sank. "Do you have files for important papers? Maybe a home safe?"

"Just some papers in a desk drawer. I haven't seen anything about that insurance." She fiddled with her wedding rings. "Warren shredded boxes and boxes of papers from our big file cabinet before we moved. Did you see it then, Warren?"

His brow furrowed. "I—I don't remember."

They'd both had health problems, both were getting older. It was entirely possible that they'd let the policy lapse.

When she'd moved back to town a month ago and they offered her free use of the cabin, she'd tried several times to get that information. But Millie had breezily waved aside her questions, saying *It is all fine* and *I'll get to it soon—I've surely got all of those papers somewhere.*

Dollar signs began rolling through Sara's brain and her nagging headache threatened to come back full force. "Don't worry about it—we'll get this all figured out. Do you remember anything about the company name? Was there a local office here in town?"

Millie suddenly brightened. "The magnet!"

"What?"

"I think there's a magnet on the fridge. It was…yellow, I think."

The refrigerator was blanketed with Post-it notes, appointment reminders, photographs and postcards. Sara began to methodically work her way through the maze of messages. At last, she found a yellow magnet with the name of an insurance company and a phone number in faded red letters. *Yes.*

She brought it to Millie. "Could this be it?"

Millie peered at it. "Maybe. It certainly looks old."

"It's Sunday, so they won't answer. But at least we can see if there's a recording so we know they're still in business." Sara punched the number into her cell phone and gripped it tightly, hoping.

The rising three-tone notes of a "Sorry, this number has been disconnected" message dashed her hopes, but she googled Hobson Insurance, Pine Bend, Montana, on her cell phone just in case.

Nothing.

Millie's face fell. "That isn't good news."

Sara gave her a quick hug. "No worries. It's possible that they changed their name or were absorbed by another company, and someone in town might know—maybe one of the other insurance adjusters. I can do some sleuthing on Monday."

"This could cost us so much money," Millie moaned. "And all because we were careless."

"I promise you, it won't cost you anything. If we can track down an insurance policy, we're golden. If not, I'll cover the repairs. It's a privilege to be living there, after all."

"But it wasn't your fault."

"You and Uncle Warren are letting me live there, and I appreciate that so much. But if you ever decide to let me buy it, you'll have no more concerns at all. No pressure— I just want you and Uncle Warren to be happy."

As usual, Millie skirted the topic with a vague wave of her hand. "If there's anything you need, be sure to tell us. You could sleep on our sofa here, if you'd like."

"Actually, there's just one little favor, but I hate to ask."

"Anything."

Sara chose her words carefully. "Well…you know that I take in pets in need. And since the fire, things are in a bit of an uproar. There's one pet that would do so much better in a quiet place like this, until I can find her a permanent home."

"Can't have dogs," Warren bellowed from his recliner.

"It's just a lonely little cat. Her owner passed away, and she's not used to a lot of commotion."

"Poor, poor thing." Millie's face filled with sympathy. "The white one?"

Sara nodded and raised her voice so Warren could hear clearly. "I promise it's not for long, and if you have any troubles I can come get her right away. I'll bring the litter box, food and litter, and keep you supplied with everything."

"Warren." There was a hint of challenge in Millie's voice, and it was clear that she wasn't really asking.

Warren got the message. He heaved a big sigh. "One cat. Just one."

"Thank you, dear," Millie whispered to Sara, her eyes sparkling. "I just *know* that little kitty needs us, and you've just made my day."

After riding three of the young horses, Tate headed over to the main ranch for Sunday dinner. Betty and Abby usually served at one o'clock, and between the two of them there was always an incredible Sunday meal on the table.

There was always a lot of laughter, as well—something so lacking while he and his brothers were growing up in this house that it seemed as if the ranch were now on a different planet. And the twins were a hoot.

Who would've guessed that Jess would turn out to be such a good dad? Those girls would be one of the things Tate missed the most after he left Montana.

But today he didn't want to linger into the midafternoon. Sara had a mess to clean up, and no one to help her. The least he could do was be neighborly.

He stepped into the kitchen through the back door, and was immediately assailed by the two little blondes who each grabbed one of his hands.

"Please, please—did you bring the puppies, Uncle Tate?" Bella cried.

"We've been waiting and waiting and *waiting*," Sophie chimed in. "Are they here?"

Abby crossed the kitchen and rested a hand on each girl's shoulder. "Let the poor man get his boots and jacket off before you assault him, girls."

They eagerly hopped from one foot to the other, their long blond ponytails dancing.

When he had his boots and jacket off he leaned down and they jumped into his arms. He pretended to wobble just a little as he straightened. "You girls are getting too big for your poor uncle Tate."

Sophie giggled, "No, we aren't. We're only in first grade."

"And we turned seven in March," Bella added proudly.

Tate raised his eyebrows. "Really? I thought you were in…oh, fifth grade. At least."

Never one to be distracted from an agenda, Bella ignored his teasing. Her rosebud mouth formed a pout. "What about the puppies, Uncle Tate?"

"They're not even a full week old, so they aren't ready to play just yet."

"But *when*?"

"Their eyes won't open until they're two weeks old. At three weeks they'll be ready to handle."

Sophie's own eyes opened wide with obvious horror. "They can't *see*? Why not?"

He tousled her ponytail. "Their eyes aren't quite finished developing, sweetie. The closed eyelids keep them safe until the eyes are ready."

Bella's face fell. "I can't play with them for another two weeks? That's a long time."

"But, you know what? I'm really going to need your help, then. They will need gentle holding and petting every day so they'll be socialized."

Sophie exchanged perplexed looks with Bella. "What's that?"

"So they'll know about people, and like to be handled. I'll bet you two will do a wonderful job."

"But we get to have them all, right? Except one for Grandma Betty?"

"I don't need a new puppy in my old age, young lady." Betty toddled into the kitchen, favoring her hip more than usual. "And you girls don't need a whole litter of puppies, either. We would be overrun with dogs."

"But, Grandma!" Sophie begged. "They need a home."

"I think it's going to storm," Betty announced, ignoring the twins' pleas on her way to the stove. "I can feel it in my bones."

"We're almost ready to eat, but then you should go lie down, Betty," Abby said as she mashed a pot of potatoes. "You've been on your feet a lot today."

Tate put the girls down and headed for the sink to wash his hands. "Tell me how I can help."

"Take the roast out of the oven and carve, if you would. Betty will make her famous roast-beef gravy, I'll put the side dishes on the table and then we should be all set. Jess will be in from the barn any minute, and Devlin is on his way."

After Tate lifted the beef onto a wood carving platter, Betty took the roasting pan and got to work on the gravy at the stove. She looked over her shoulder at him. "Missed you at church this morning."

"I didn't know when Sara would show up, and whether or not she would need some help. She doesn't have family around her anymore. By the time she came it was too late to go, so I just worked a couple more horses."

Betty looked out the window with a faraway expression. "When you were growing up, I made sure all three of you boys attended church and Sunday school every weekend."

"I remember. If we were all quiet and paid attention, you took us to the little café on Main Street for frosted donuts and chocolate milk."

She chuckled at the memory. "There were three of you and one of me, so I wasn't above a bit of bribery. I figured the good Lord would understand."

He started carving slices of the succulent, juicy roast. "I remember the drives home to the ranch too. You always peppered us with questions about the service. The kid with the most points got out of doing dishes the rest of the day."

"You boys really kept me on my toes. I had to listen real hard myself, just to stay one step ahead of you three." She finished whisking the gravy, adjusted the seasoning and poured it into a gravy boat Tate remembered washing as a kid.

"I'll be there next Sunday, I promise."

"Where is your friend? I thought she would be here by now. I hope everything's all right."

"Who?"

"Sara. You did invite her for dinner, right? I'm sure she has her hands full without trying to cook too."

"From the sounds of things she had a busy day planned, so I didn't ask."

Betty waved a ladle in his direction. "The poor girl has enough to do as it is. We'll have plenty of leftovers, so after we're done you can bring her some."

He'd already offered to stop by to help, but she hadn't been all that receptive. He smiled to himself.

Now he had the perfect excuse.

Chapter Seven

Sara stood at the open doorway and watched the fire chief poke and prod his way through the charred interior of the garage.

Nightfall had been closing in when he'd examined the damage yesterday, but in the light of day it was easier to see the full picture. It didn't look good.

His clipboard in hand, Gene joined her outside. "Your insurance adjuster will give you an evaluation of the damage to the garage," he said, flipping through his notes. "I'd guess it's a total loss. If it were mine, I wouldn't even try to cobble it all back together. I would bulldoze it, and start over. And for sure, I'd hire an electrician to come out and inspect the wiring in the cabin itself."

"My uncle told me he had a lot of tools in the garage."

"He must have been quite a craftsman. He had a lot of mighty-fine equipment. His chisels and wrenches are probably all right. You can rake through the rubble to see what you find." Gene pursed his lips and shook his head slowly in sympathy. "But the power tools are all toast."

"I can only imagine how much they cost."

Gene rubbed his chin. "He might be able to salvage the table saw—it was in the corner with the least fire damage.

But I wouldn't worry too much. Insurance should cover the contents, at least to a certain extent—the adjuster will let you know."

Warren was in poor health now, gradually needing more physical assistance. He would likely never be able to work in his shop again, but she already dreaded telling him about the loss. "And what about the cause of the fire—did you find anything different?"

"Nope. The greatest amount of fire damage was behind the electrical panel, so I figure that was the origin. I saw no evidence of arson."

Sara drew in a sharp breath. "I hadn't even thought of that."

He shrugged. "If you were in a city, expert investigators could come out, but this situation seems pretty obvious to me."

"You've probably lived in the area for a long time, right?"

"Almost twenty years. I manage the feed mill in town." He glanced at his watch and jangled the truck keys in his pocket. "I'd better be off. The missus said she'd have Sunday dinner on the table at two."

"Just one thing—do you remember a Hobson Insurance Company in Pine Bend?"

He rocked back on his heels, thinking. "Doesn't sound familiar, but you could ask the insurance people on the corner of Main and Third. They might know."

Sara shook his hand. "Again—many thanks. I appreciate everything you've done."

Gene had been gone only a few minutes when she heard the sound of a diesel pickup rumbling up the long drive, then Tate's black truck appeared.

Her pulse kicked up a notch as she finished filling a bucket of warm water at the kitchen sink, added a quick spritz of dishwashing soap and went out on the porch to meet him. "Honest, I know you're busy. You didn't need to come over again."

"Oh yes, I did. Grandma's orders." He reached into the backseat and withdrew several overfilled canvas shopping bags, then headed toward the cabin. "She thought you might be starving."

She opened the door for him and followed him to the kitchen. "Something smells amazing. What do you have in there?"

"Enough for an army. Or at least, enough to cover you for a few days. It's all still warm, so you can have your lunch now and refrigerate the rest." He chuckled as he started pulling out one foil nine-by-thirteen pan after another. "Roast beef, mashed potatoes and gravy, glazed baby carrots, a couple of salads, a few dozen chocolate-chip cookies, and what looks like an apple—no, a cherry pie."

She stared at the growing array on the counter. "Wow. Have you eaten yet? We should share."

"I already had dinner with the family, so this is all yours. Betty said she made doubles of everything." Surveying the interior of the cabin, his gaze landed on the two small tabletop fans she'd set up to exhaust smoky air through the open windows. "Did you look for some industrial-size fans?"

"I called around, but couldn't find anyplace that was open on a Saturday evening or Sunday. My two little fans are helping, though."

He thought for a moment, then pulled his phone from his pocket and tapped in a speed-dial number. He smiled after he disconnected the call. "There are a couple thirty-inch floor fans at Jess's place. They keep the horses more comfortable in the horse barns when we travel to shows during the summer. Jess is bringing them over."

"I could've gone to get them," she protested. "I don't mean to be a bother."

"Helping someone is never a bother. So, where should I start?"

"Really, I don't—"

He spied the task list on a clipboard she'd left on the kitchen counter, spun it around to face him and began reading aloud. "Scrub walls. Floors. Counters and cupboards. Maybe repaint ceiling? Wash all linens and clothing. Search the garage for salvageable tools and supplies. Find insurance company."

He stopped reading and looked up at her. "*Find* the company?"

"Yeah. Well—I hope so. Warren and Millie don't remember if they accidentally let the insurance lapse, and apparently they have no paperwork, because Warren had a big shredding party before they moved to town. Millie says he was shredding for hours, so who knows what else he might have destroyed. They aren't even sure about which company it was. I'm going to try to track down the one name they remember, but I'm guessing the policy lapsed."

"So what then?" he asked quietly.

"They don't have the cash, that's for sure. Hopefully they'll let me buy the place sooner or later, and then I'll rebuild the garage."

He whistled under his breath. "You know that won't be cheap, right?"

"I googled it this morning. Just the materials could be around six grand or more, and with the labor, maybe three times that." She shrugged. "So you're right, it won't be cheap. But it is what it is, and at least there's already a concrete slab. I don't know about reusing a steel roof."

"Wait on any decisions until you talk to me. Jess probably knows the best construction people around here, or would know who to ask." He ran a finger down her list. "I'll work on the garage. Is that all right with you? We're supposed to be getting more snow, and you don't want it filling up with a big drift."

"Perfect. Thanks, Tate. For everything."

"No trouble at all."

He looked up at the high ceiling and frowned, then grabbed his Stetson at the front door. "I'm bringing in an extension ladder. We'll need it for the walls."

"Thanks." She surveyed the cabin, glad it wasn't any larger, and caught a sneeze on her forearm. "At least there isn't any soot on the walls, but I can't believe how much smoke came under the door to the garage. It smells awful in here."

Taking the bucket of warm water to the far end of the kitchen, she sprinkled baking soda on a damp sponge and began scrubbing one section at a time, then cleaned it off with a damp cloth.

After rubbing it dry with an old towel she moved to the next section, laboriously cleaning and wiping and drying until her shoulders started to ache. She stood and stretched, her hands at the small of her back, and surveyed the rest of the cabin in dismay.

After an hour, she hadn't yet completed even one side of the kitchen. This was going to take *forever*.

She turned at the sound of boots clomping up the steps to the porch. "Hey, Tate—how's it going?"

But it wasn't Tate. It was Jess, followed by Abby, Devlin and a slender woman with wavy, deep auburn hair. They were all carrying buckets and armfuls of rags.

"I brought the fans and some extra helpers," Jess said. "Abby, Devlin and Devlin's fiancée, Chloe. Her dad was a foreman at the ranch when we were growing up, so you might have seen her in elementary school."

Chloe stepped forward with a warm smile. "We just lived here for five years, though, and I had bright red hair back then. So you probably don't remember me."

Sara studied her as the memories slowly filtered back. "You had freckles back then, just a scattering over your nose, and the prettiest curly hair I'd ever seen. Right? I didn't have either, and I was so jealous."

Chloe laughed. "My hair was *always* tangled, because after mom left, my cowhand dad had no clue about what to do with a little girl's hair. And I *hated* those freckles because Jess and Dev used to tease me. Now I wish I still had them, but they've disappeared and my hair got darker. No one in town recognized me when I came back."

Devlin drew her close to his side and kissed her cheek. "If I hadn't thought you were so cute I wouldn't have teased you. Promise."

"This is a really nice place," Abby murmured as she turned around to survey the cabin. "Beautiful cabinetry, and I love all the windows. I didn't even know this place existed, until Tate told us about it. You sure don't have to worry about neighbors up here."

Sara smiled. "Just you Langfords and a lot of wildlife— the shared property line is a hundred yards to the west. But I promise I'll keep the noise down."

Devlin lifted the bucket in his hand. "So, where do we start?"

"Honestly, I should just offer you coffee for coming all the way here. I don't want to put you all to work."

"That's why we came," Abby said. "Betty is watching the twins, so this is like a mini vacation for me. Just tell us what to do so we can get busy. We've got to be home at five so Betty can go into town for bingo at the Senior Center."

Sara explained the cleaning process she'd found on the internet, and everyone got to work on a different area of the cabin. After Jess and Tate appeared with the fans and set them up, it was too noisy to chat, so everyone just kept working.

Sara was crouched in a corner of the kitchen when she saw Tate's boots at the corner of her eye. She glanced past him to the clock on the wall. "Four thirty already? How did that happen?"

She stood, her knees creaking after she'd been hunched over for so long. The others were gathering their supplies and pulling on their jackets.

"We made some headway," Abby called out over the noise of the fans. "This whole west-facing great room wall is done."

"It looks really nice," Chloe added. "Just look at the beautiful grain of that wood."

"You're right. The place was empty for a long time, and I didn't realize how dingy the walls were until now." Sara made a face. "I can sure see where I need to start working next."

The day had been sunny and bright, in the fifties, but now the nighttime chill was settling in. Sara turned off the fans and shut the windows.

Devlin and Chloe came over to give Sara a quick farewell hug before going out the door.

Abby lingered. "You're coming back to stay with us tonight, right? I'll be in California for the next two weeks, but Betty is there. You're welcome anytime, and for as long as you'd like."

"I really appreciate the offer, Abby. But I'd better stay

and keep at this late as I can. I work all week and won't have much time. I'm sure Tate is getting tired of all of my animals at his place."

Tate strolled in as Devlin and Chloe left. "I heard that, and it's no trouble at all. But can you send me a text on what to feed them and how much? Then you won't need to stop by twice a day."

"Well, I—"

"Done. Can you come outside? I'd like to show you what Jess and I have been doing and ask you some questions."

She gave a helpless laugh. Dealing with this generation of Langfords was like trying to corral a hurricane. Without their willingness to pitch in, everything would have been so much harder. *Thank you, Lord, for sending me all of this help.*

Jess stood in front of the garage, studying the opening. He looked over his shoulder at her approach. "Given the structural damage, you wouldn't want to park a vehicle inside, in case it collapses."

She nodded. "No argument there. I'm just glad my truck wasn't inside during the fire."

"We found sheets of plywood in that little barn. If you don't mind, we could nail them up so the front of the garage will be closed against bad weather and vermin. It won't look pretty, though."

"Sounds absolutely perfect."

"Good, I'll drive my truck over and get the plywood while Tate asks you about a few things."

Twilight was descending, rendering the interior of the garage in a monochrome palette of shades of black and gray.

"You should stay clear too. It's not all that safe in there." Tate pointed to several stacked boxes. "We've been raking through the cinders, and the all-metal hand tools like wrenches and chisels are in those boxes. The fire chief probably already told you that the power tools were basically incinerated—the motors, cords and any plastic housing."

She nodded.

"Jess and I were talking, and we know you haven't yet found out if there's insurance coverage. If there isn't, we'd be willing to round up a crew of friends to rebuild the garage. If the Amish can raise an entire barn in a day, surely we can put up a simple structure like this. You'd just need to supply the materials and hire an electrician."

The garage situation had been weighing heavily on her heart ever since she'd heard Warren and Millie waffle about their insurance coverage.

That the Langfords had been so willing to help her stunned her. Gus was a different story, but had she been wrong about the rest of his family all this time?

"Th-thank you. I—I—" Tate shot a grin at her that made her feel strangely breathless. "I don't know what to say."

"Just being neighborly." He touched the brim of his Stetson. "I thought maybe you'd sleep a little easier knowing you weren't going to sink deeper into debt."

Speechless at his unexpected thoughtfulness, she watched him stride out to his truck, unable to look away.

She'd moved back to Pine Bend with no intention of wasting time on any flirtations. That simply wasn't in her game plan—not when she needed to work hard and make every minute count. But she'd certainly never expected to encounter Tate again, much less find that she felt the same old awareness simmering through her, just like it had in high school.

Yesterday, he'd even called her honey, but while her

heart had warmed at his caring touch, those courtly cowboy manners were probably so commonplace in his life that they meant nothing at all. He'd always been a magnet for all of the pretty girls who flocked to him at school. By now, an inveterate charmer like him had probably left a hundred broken hearts in his wake and never even realized it.

But when he'd flinched and turned away at her simple kiss of thanks, that told her all she needed to know. She didn't need to worry about avoiding any awkward complications, because he had no interest in her at all.

On Monday morning Sara awoke early, hurried to Tate's place to feed all of her animals and pick up the white cat, then drove to her clinic for a solid morning of appointments.

When the clinic closed for lunch at noon she collected the cat from a cage in the back room, put her in a carrier and gathered some supplies, then drove down Main Street to Third Avenue.

Sure enough, there was the office Gene had mentioned—Frost & Sons Insurance Company. Sara hurried inside and waited at the front desk while an early-twentysomething woman chattered into her cell phone.

She pulled her cell phone away from her ear and looked up at Sara from beneath her bright purple bangs. "Can I help you?"

"Just two quick things—I'm sure it's your lunch break too. My aunt and uncle think they had policies with a Hobson Insurance here in town. Does that ring a bell?"

Her brow furrowed. "Nope."

Swiveling in her chair, she reached for a Rolodex on a cluttered credenza and started flipping through the address cards. She got to the end and checked once again, then shook her head. "Just a minute."

She craned her neck toward a closed door behind her. "Mr. Tompkins? Someone here to see you."

A chair squeaked, and a dapper man in his midsixties opened the door. He smiled. "Did I hear the name Hobson? Franklin passed on seven years ago, and then I took over. This was once his office, though."

"My aunt and uncle—Warren and Millie Branson— think they have a homeowner's policy with that company. Obviously it would have lapsed by now, unless it carried forward to you."

"Hmm. Their name does sound familiar." He nodded and waved her into his office, where he settled behind his desk and started tapping his keyboard. After a few minutes he leaned back in his chair. "They took out a policy eight years ago on a cabin up in the foothills. It was insured through Hobson, and they continued their coverage with me after I took over. But eleven months ago they ignored three reminder emails, a letter and a phone call, so the policy lapsed."

"About the time they were heading into their decline," she said softly.

"Hmm?"

"I don't suppose there's any recourse—back payments, or something? Extensions for long-term clients?"

He chuckled. "Afraid not. Not after almost a year."

She stood and shook his hand. "Thanks for your time."

"If I can ever talk to you about your own insurance needs, be sure to stop by." He walked her to the front door.

"We've got to get the cabin reinsured and I need to look at renter's insurance, as well, soon as possible. Can I get some quotes over the phone?" She nabbed a business card from the secretary's desk. "I have another errand and need to get back to work."

At Millie and Warren's apartment Sara took a deep breath and knocked.

When Millie opened her door, her face instantly wreathed with joy. She bent down to peer into the small carrier. "She is beautiful!"

"Don't need a cat," Warren grumbled from his recliner. "If you don't have a barn, you don't need a cat."

"Oh, you never mind him," Millie said in a conspiratorial whisper. "Give him five days and he'll be doting on this cat like an old mother hen."

"If he doesn't come around, just call me and I'll be back to pick her up." Sara stepped back out into the hallway and brought in the kitty litter, domed litter box and bags of dry cat food, then got everything set up. "I'll be bringing you everything she needs. But if you ever need to buy some food choose only the high-quality food—not the cheap brands."

Millie beamed when Sara opened the door of the carrier and the cat strode out, tail high, as regal as any queen. "I hope she'll be friendly."

"It might take her some time to adjust, but she's been very sweet with me."

"I think I'll call her Princess." Millie reached down to stroke her, but the cat took off and raced into the bedroom, where something crashed to the floor, then she zoomed around the living room, ricocheted off the back of the sofa and took a flying leap to land square on Warren's paunchy belly.

"Ooof!" He stared at the apparition in front of him. She stared right back, her tail twitching. "You should call this thing Smoke. She smells like a cigarette ashtray."

"She was in the cabin during the fire, Uncle Warren."

Sara crossed the room to take the cat from his lap, but Princess—or Smoke—moved higher up his chest and curled contently just below his chin.

She reached for the cat again, but Warren lifted a hand. "She can stay," he grumbled, sounding entirely out of sorts, but he settled a hand on her fur and began rubbing gently behind her ear. "Hhhmpff. Not much of a lady. She purrs like a boat motor needing a tune-up."

"Cats always seem to go for the people who like them least," Millie whispered with a small smile. "It's like they're trying to make a point."

"Or," Sara countered quietly, "maybe they can sense who likes them but doesn't want to show it. I think she won him over in less than thirty seconds."

She glanced at her watch, then moved closer to Warren so they both could hear her better. "I need to get back to the clinic, but just wanted you to know that I checked on the Hobson Insurance Company. That fellow died, but another agent took over the office space. It's called Frost & Sons now. You were on automatic annual payments until you changed bank accounts. Your cabin policy lapsed almost a year ago."

Warren sat up a little higher in his chair. "So what does that mean, exactly?"

"Thanks to the fire wall you built, the cabin wasn't damaged at all—other than a lot of smoke. I'm working on cleaning it up to get rid of the smell. But the garage is a total loss. There is no insurance money to cover it."

He looked up at her. "My tools?"

"Basically everything is a loss except for some chisels and wrenches—and maybe one fancy table saw that could be repaired."

He gave a gusty sigh. "I built that garage myself and until a few years ago I could have done it again. But not

"FAST FIVE" READER SURVEY

Your participation entitles you to:
✳ Up to 4 FREE BOOKS and Thank-You Gifts Worth Over $20!

Complete the survey in minutes.

Romance

Suspense

Get Up to 4 **FREE Books**

Your Thank-You Gifts include up to **4 FREE BOOKS** and **2 Mystery Gifts**. There's no obligation to purchase anything!

See inside for details.

Please help make our
"Fast Five" Reader Survey
a success!

Dear Reader,

Since you are a lover of our books, your opinions are important to us... and so is your time.

That's why we made sure your **"FAST FIVE" READER SURVEY** can be completed in just a few minutes. Your answers to the five questions will help us remain at the forefront of women's fiction.

And, as a thank-you for participating, we'd like to send you up to **4 FREE BOOKS** and **FREE THANK-YOU GIFTS!**

Try **Love Inspired® Romance Larger-Print** books featuring Christian characters facing modern-day challenges.

Try **Love Inspired® Suspense Larger-Print** novels featuring Christian characters facing challenges to their faith... and lives.

Or TRY BOTH!

Enjoy your gifts with our appreciation,

Pam Powers

To get up to
4 FREE BOOKS & THANK-YOU GIFTS:

✳ Quickly complete the "Fast Five" Reader Survey
and return the insert.

"FAST FIVE" READER SURVEY

1 Do you sometimes read a book a second or third time? ○ Yes ○ No

2 Do you often choose reading over other forms of entertainment such as television? ○ Yes ○ No

3 When you were a child, did someone regularly read aloud to you? ○ Yes ○ No

4 Do you sometimes take a book with you when you travel outside the home? ○ Yes ○ No

5 In addition to books, do you regularly read newspapers and magazines? ○ Yes ○ No

YES! Please send me my Free Rewards, consisting of **2 Free Books from each series I select** and **Free Mystery Gifts**. I understand that I am under no obligation to buy anything, as explained on the back of this card.

❏ **Love Inspired® Romance Larger-Print** (122/322 IDL GNSN)
❏ **Love Inspired® Suspense Larger-Print** (107/307 IDL GNSN)
❏ **Try Both** (122/322 & 107/307 IDL GNSY)

FIRST NAME	LAST NAME

ADDRESS

APT.#	CITY

STATE/PROV.   ZIP/POSTAL CODE

READER SERVICE—Here's how it works:

anymore. And I don't have the money to have it done right."

"I've…um…actually had a really generous offer of help. Some local folks said they could—"

"Who?"

"Neighbors," she hedged. "If the materials are supplied, they've offered to rebuild it."

Millie twisted her fingers together. "But those materials would still cost more than we could pay. Right, Warren?"

Warren glowered at Sara. "*Which* neighbors?"

"The Langfords. Jess, Devlin and Tate—if he's still around. They thought they could—"

Warren's eyes sparked fire. "I won't be a charity case. Not for the likes of them."

Sara soldiered on as if she hadn't heard. "They thought they could get some of their friends together too. They just wouldn't do any of the electrical work."

Warren's chin jerked up in silent defiance.

"One last thing—the cabin needs home insurance. It ought to be my responsibility and I can take care of it today, if you don't mind."

Millie frowned at her husband, her lips pressed tightly together. "You go ahead, dear, but give us the bill. No sense losing the cabin too. But as I've said before, you need to stay clear of that family. Every last one of them. Warren always said you couldn't trust 'em far as you could throw them, and he was right."

"But, Aunt Millie—"

Her aunt took her hand, led her into the bedroom and shut the door. Millie took a little upholstered chair in the corner and motioned for Sara to sit on the edge of the bed.

"I know you have a good heart, but you weren't in Pine Bend when we lost the ranch. There are things you need to know."

"I know the bank foreclosed because of debt—and maybe Gus was behind it," Sara said slowly. "And I know Warren begged the banker for an extension that was denied."

"That's all true. But we were behind by just two months, and Warren told the bank that we would have a load of cattle to ship in sixty days, which would have more than covered it."

"They wouldn't hold off just a little longer?"

"They could have. It was an entirely arbitrary decision by the banker, but he had that right and he used it. A friend of Warren's told him Gus was at the bank time and again, behind closed doors, demanding some kind of favor…and within a week the banker called in our loans. The timing couldn't have been worse—late winter, when we had no crops or hay to sell, and no cattle ready for market," Millie said bitterly. "We could never prove it, but I think the timing was planned. Then the auction was scheduled quickly, with little promotion."

"I'm so sorry, Aunt Millie. Truly."

"Gus picked up our ranch for a song and managed to get most of the livestock and equipment for pennies on the dollar. Few people figured they could win the bidding against him, so when they realized he was there, snapping everything up, they didn't even try. I will never forget his smug expression when he looked at us at the end of the day, while he was getting into his fancy truck."

"But his boys had all moved away from home by then. Right? None of this was their fault."

"Maybe I'm wrong, but I'm sure I saw one of them helping the auctioneer—hauling things out of the barn. We only took the furnishings that would fit in the cabin, and watching him dragging our things out of the house to be sold for pennies just broke my heart."

Sara had known the basic facts, but until now she

hadn't felt the full impact of what had happened. How quickly and callously a whole lifetime of hard work could be swept away.

She moved closer and reached out to take Millie's hand. "I'm so sorry."

Millie sighed heavily. "We heard neighbors crowing about how cheaply they bought this thing or that, and we watched our entire lives go under the auctioneer's gavel as if it meant nothing to anyone. It might have been better if we'd stayed away."

"If I'd only known, I could have come back. Tried to help somehow. Why didn't you call me? Or write?"

Millie rested her other hand on top of Sara's. "What could you have done? You needed to be in school. Nothing would have stopped Gus Langford at that point. He'd already snapped up the Cavanaughs' ranch, and he knew what he was about."

"But my parents should have stepped in. Surely they could've given you a loan or…or something." Sara tried to quell the bitter tone in her voice. "Did they even offer?"

"Your uncle Warren is a proud man. He didn't even mention it to your dad until it was too late."

"They still should have tried."

Millie sighed. "Yes—your dad and mom offered to help. But what they could offer didn't come close to what it would've taken. And Warren refused to be beholden to his brother, at any rate."

Sara had put her phone on Silent when she arrived, but now she felt it buzzing a second time in her pocket. She pulled it out to take a look. The clinic had texted twice, and she was now a half hour late.

"I'm so sorry, Aunt Millie—I've got to get back. I've got clients waiting." She stood and leaned over to kiss her aunt's weathered cheek. "I can come back after work, though, if you'd like. I hate leaving you now after all you've said. Are you all right?"

"Tough as a wild turkey hen," Millie said firmly, though her lower lip trembled and her hands were shaking. "But you needed to hear the *full* story before anyone tries to tell you different. We want nothing to do with any of them."

Sara bit her lower lip. "The sons were gone by that time. Tate told me that they all wanted to *escape* their father and that ranch."

"Those boys were raised by that man—and whether by nurture or nature, they are what he made them."

Sara chose her words carefully. "But...is that fair? Can't people change?"

"Mixing with the Langfords isn't something we do, or want to hear about. It brings up grief we'd just as soon forget. You'd best not ever bring up that name in front of Warren again."

Late into the night, as Sara cleaned another section of the cabin, she could still hear the edge in Millie's voice. The unmistakable thread of warning.

Her aunt and uncle had been terribly wounded. That wasn't going to change. And it was pretty clear that they were never going to forgive Gus or his family.

It wasn't fair, and it wasn't right.

But did Sara now need to make a choice, between the only true, loving family she had left and any association with Tate and the other Langfords?

It should be an easy decision.

With her troubled family history, family had always mattered most. It *always* came first, because she knew just how precious absolute and unequivocal love was.

So why did she feel as if her heart was breaking in two?

Chapter Eight

Tate poured himself another cup of coffee, stood staring out the kitchen window for a long while, then settled at his kitchen table with his laptop and a notebook to continue working on estimates for house renovations.

The clock was ticking. He needed to make every day count if he was going to accomplish all of his goals at the ranch before leaving for the rodeo contractor's auction in May.

He was working the young horses in the arena daily. He'd finished checking the fence line on Monday, then went into town on Tuesday to order new windows for the second-floor bedrooms and pick up fencing materials.

Mid-March was a couple weeks away and then the spring thaw would be just around the corner. Once he finished repairing the fencing around the Branson property, it could be fully utilized in the summer pasture rotation.

One big project checked off his list, to help out his brothers.

He almost wished he had more time in Montana. But it wasn't a choice. Not with one perfect chance to get back into the rodeo life that had become as much a part of his existence as breathing.

A low growl and a single woof sounded from the nest box installed in the far corner for Lucy and her pups. He saw her peer over the top of the box, then drop back down to her family. "You hear something, girl?"

He looked out the window again, but the driveway and parking area were still empty.

He could tell that Sara had been here to take care of her animals twice a day, but since Sunday evening he'd either missed her entirely, or just caught sight of her as she was leaving. If he didn't know better, he'd think she was trying to avoid him. But why would that be?

He couldn't think of a single thing he'd said or done to rile her when he'd brought his family to her place on Sunday to help out for a while. In fact, she'd *kissed* him.

He'd been so taken aback that he hadn't reacted quickly enough—and even now, he wished he could relive the moment and return that innocent, sweet kiss with one that was longer, with his arms around her...like the ones he remembered from years ago.

But maybe she regretted that impulsive expression of thanks.

Today was finally Thursday, though, and he would get to see her again for sure. She had an appointment at nine to see the injured gelding one last time and vaccinate the barn cats.

The cats were caught. The gelding was in his stall. And hopefully, Tate would have some answers of his own.

Ten minutes later he heard the crunch of tires on gravel and saw her truck pull up to the barn. He pulled on his boots, grabbed his coat and headed out the door.

She turned at his approach with a look of surprise. "I didn't see your truck, so I didn't think you were here."

"I haven't unloaded my fencing supplies yet, so I

parked it in the machine shed. I hear we're supposed to get some snow tonight."

He followed her into the horse barn and brought the injured colt out of his stall. "I think he's looking really good. I long-lined him in the indoor arena at a jog for just a few minutes yesterday and he didn't favor that leg at all."

"Can you walk him up and down the aisle for me so I can see him move?"

He led the colt halfway down the aisle, then turned back. Sara's gaze stayed riveted on the colt's forelegs until he pulled to a stop in front of her.

She nodded. "You're right. He is looking good. Can you cross-tie him?"

She bent down by the colt's leg and began unwrapping the bandages. She looked up at Tate and smiled. "You've done a good job. He's healing nicely. I'm going to leave the bandaging off now. I wouldn't turn him outside with the other horses just yet, but you can start long-lining him daily and loping is fine. I don't need to see him again, but wait a couple more weeks before he goes outside with the others."

"Good. So next up is the cat rodeo. Are you ready? I can't guarantee that they're going to cooperate."

She gathered up the bandages and dropped them in a trash can outside the tack room while Tate put the colt back in his stall. "Do I need to watch for escapees if I open this door?"

"No problem. All three of the barn cats are in pet carriers. I didn't feed them last night, so they all came for breakfast this morning and I nabbed them."

She opened the door and stepped inside.

Theodore's cage was farther back in the room, away from any chilly drafts, but the bird saw her right away and began a lively two-step back and forth in his cage to the tune of one of his rap songs.

"Hello, pretty bird," she murmured to him. "I hope you can come home soon."

Tate stood at her shoulder and looked into the cage. "How are things going at your cabin?"

"Fair. I had long days at the clinic Monday, Tuesday and Wednesday, and didn't get home until late. But I've been doing loads of laundry a second time, to try to get rid of the smoke, and hope to wrap up the cleaning over the weekend."

"If you want the Langford crew to come back we'd be happy to help—except Abby's in California. And I hear Chloe probably won't be back from Butte this weekend, either."

"Thanks, but I can take care of the rest by myself."

"It's no trouble. Are you sure?"

She seemed to waver, her eyes troubled, then she shook her head, her lips pressed in a firm line. "No need. None at all."

Leaning forward, she cooed to the parrot. "Even with all that's been done, I might always smell faint, residual smoke in that cabin, though. I'll probably need to take Theodore to the vet clinic long term."

"What about the dogs and cats?"

"They should be okay once I'm done. But smoke is extremely toxic to birds—their lungs, skin, eyes…and even their feet, if they perch on something that's contaminated. I'm amazed at how well he fared after the fire."

"At least he wasn't perching up in the loft where the smoke was heavier."

"I'm so glad you found him hiding in the farthest corner away from smoke. I used an anti-inflammatory and bronchodilators on him for the first couple days, which probably helped."

He lifted one of the carriers onto the round table in front of the picture window looking out into the arena. "Here's barn cat number one—the calico. None of them have been handled much, far as I know. So good luck."

She lifted the cat from its carrier, checked its ears for mites, vaccinated it for rabies and FVRCP for other common diseases, then squeezed a single-dose tube of flea product onto the skin between its shoulder blades. She next gave the thoroughly disgruntled cat a worming pill and set it free.

Tate laughed. "That cat shot out of here like a rocket."

Picking up the next carrier, she lifted out the gold-and-white cat, and when she was done, she angled a subdued smile in Tate's direction. "That first one will probably hide and sulk for a day or so."

He watched her gently examine, vaccinate and treat the final barn cat, a black-and-gray-striped tabby. "Did you find out anything about the insurance on the cabin?"

"Lapsed, unfortunately. But I've reinsured the cabin in Warren's and Millie's names and started renter's insurance for myself." She finished with the cat and let it go, but it lingered and rubbed its head against her arm before gracefully leaping off the table.

"You were worried about your uncle being upset by any bad news."

She lifted a shoulder in a slight shrug. "He took…most of the news pretty well."

"Did you talk to him about rebuilding the garage?"

"Briefly."

"Did you tell him his old neighbors would be willing to help?"

"It was very kind of you to offer, but at this point I think rebuilding will be a long ways off." She didn't meet Tate's eyes as she watched the final barn cat meander toward the door. "Thanks again for letting me keep all of my rescues here. I promise to move them back to my cabin this coming weekend."

If she did, he would miss these random chances for conversations with her. The occasional glimpses of her here at the ranch, in her trim navy jacket with the Pine Bend Vet logo embroidered across the back, her pretty blond ponytail swinging from the back of her ball cap.

The thought filled him with an inexplicable sense of loss.

"Why don't you just leave them all here awhile longer? Then you can take all the time you need with your cabin."

"Well…"

"I'll miss all of your dogs and cats if they go," he added gravely. "Especially…um…the parrot."

"Now I *know* you're not telling the truth." A brief smile touched her lips. "I've commandeered two of your box stalls and most of your tack room—and I noticed you've had to put a couple of horses in another barn because of it."

"No problem. The dogs should stay in here where it's warmer. And of course the parrot needs the heated tack room. He couldn't be anywhere else."

She mulled over his offer for a moment. "Maybe just another week? But let me pay you for your trouble, then. That would only be fair."

"Definitely not. And if your rescues need to stay even longer, so be it." He followed her out to her vet truck and opened the back door for her so she could stow her equipment. "Though there is one thing. A small favor?"

"Name it."

"Jess and Devlin thought the house should be bull-dozed."

She flinched. "You're kidding."

"They weren't. But I like a home with a sense of history, and I think it's a gem worth saving."

She tipped her head and looked up at him. "Really?"

"I've got only so much time here in Montana, though. I promised them I'd do as much as I could on the renovation and leave detailed plans for the rest, but it's hard to know where to start and what updates should be done. You spent a lot of time here while growing up, so you might have much better ideas than me."

She looked past him to the house, with its sagging porch and peeling paint. "There was so much love in that house, once. It deserves another chance."

"So you'll help? Just a couple evenings is all I ask. Maybe starting tomorrow?"

"I will. And I think I still owe you a dinner too." She climbed behind the wheel and started the engine.

"Wait—" He'd never been a touchy-feely-emotional sort of guy, and it took him a second to find the right words. "You seem…different. Is anything wrong?"

She rested a wrist on the top of the steering wheel, and stared through the windshield. It took her a long time to answer. "Nothing, really," she said finally. "Nothing at all."

But long after her truck bounced down the lane and out of sight, he stared after her and wondered why she hadn't told the truth.

By the time Sara finished the rest of her ranch calls for the day, it was almost six o'clock and pitch-black outside with just a few random flakes of snow swirling in front of her headlights.

When she stopped to take care of her animals at Tate's place she lingered at the big window in the tack room and watched him work a young paint under the bright fluorescent arena lights.

If she'd ever given thought to the skills of a saddle bronc competitor, they certainly wouldn't have equated to what she was seeing now.

Not that she knew much about rodeo, but with the broncs and bulls it seemed to be all about staying aboard for eight seconds while adding as much flash and drama as possible to drive up the score.

But now, Tate was sitting nearly motionless in the saddle as he rode at a lope, as if he and the young gelding were a single, fluid entity, his hands low and relaxed, the reins loose. The colt's head was held low, his tail drifted quietly behind him—with no signs of tail wringing or head-tossing agitation, even when Tate slowed him to walk and circled the arena a half-dozen times.

Sara could tell the colt was turning out beautifully in Tate's kind and experienced hands.

Would Warren and Millie think any different of Tate if they could actually *see* his gentleness? See how kind and thoughtful he'd been toward her since the fire? Or would they simply harden their hearts and see only what they wanted to—the son of the man who had selfishly turned their lives upside down?

She didn't have to wonder; Millie had already made her feelings clear, and even now Sara felt as if a rock had settled in her midsection.

It was so unfair to be caught in the middle of a bad situation. But how could she choose friendship with Tate over the two people in the world who loved her most?

Tate stopped in the middle of the arena, backed the colt a dozen feet or so, then dismounted, flipped the stirrup over the saddle seat and loosened the girth.

She turned away to finish feeding Theodore and the

cats, and took food and water to all of the dogs. She had almost slipped out the barn door when she heard the clip-clop of horse shoes on cement at the far end of the horse barn.

"How was your afternoon?" Tate cross-tied the gelding and began unsaddling him. "Anything exciting?"

She turned, wishing she hadn't lingered quite so long at the window. "Just the usual—and busy."

"Since you're here anyway, would you like to go up to the house and take a quick look around? It might give you something to ponder before we get together tomorrow night."

"I...well, I guess so."

"I still need to feed the horses, so feel free to check it out. I need to warn you, though. I suspect it's not at all like you remember."

Curious now, she nodded. "If you don't mind."

A wry smile deepened the dimple in his left cheek that she'd always thought impossibly charming. "Have at it. There's a new spiral notebook on the kitchen table, if you'd like to jot down some notes, though I can guarantee there are things you will not forget. Ever."

She reached for the doorknob. "I don't know if I should be scared, or just curious."

"Maybe both. See what you think. I moved Lucy and her bed into the little storage room off the kitchen, just so you know. You probably won't see her, though. The pups aren't yet two weeks old and she rarely leaves them."

The breeze had kicked up since Sara arrived, and snow-flakes were spinning beneath the high security light illuminating the parking area in front of the barns. She zipped her jacket all the way up and bowed her head as she jogged to the house.

Even from the outside it looked sad and neglected,

with the old white picket fence sagging in places and the gate hanging from one hinge. The steps up to the porch creaked, and one even had a gaping hole.

Inside the front door she reached blindly to the left side until her fingertips connected with a set of light switches.

The cut-glass light fixture above bathed the entryway in golden light. The old oak woodwork was still there, though as she stepped farther into the living room she saw water damage on the wallpaper and dark water stains on the ceiling.

Taking a steadying breath she moved on through the dining room and into the kitchen.

A flood of memories rushed through her at the curling yellow linoleum and the yellowed Formica countertops. The white wood cabinets, the paint worn off around each knob.

How many birthday cakes had Millie made at these counters? How many cookies and pies and other wonderful treats? But these walls were watermarked, as well, and the ceiling was sagging.

The more she saw, the more she realized Devlin and Jess were right—there might be good reason to just tear the house down. A cold breeze whistled through the windows and in some rooms, mildew and mold made her sneeze. Unlike a modern open-concept design, the floor plan was cut up into small rooms that limited the placement of furniture and use of space.

Yet in every room memories curled around her like a soft sepia mist, and she found herself wistfully running her fingertips along the woodwork, wishing she could relive those wonderful times.

Millie's rocker had been here—where she knitted and crocheted and read her magazines. And there was the place Warren had sat in his easy chair and watched the farm-and-ranch news on the TV.

Tate came inside just as she was headed up the open staircase. He shucked off his boots and coat and came to the bottom of the stairs. "The banister is pretty wobbly. Be careful."

The three bedrooms upstairs still sported the same floral wallpaper Millie had always loved, though now some of it was hanging in tatters where there had been leaks in the ceiling. Two of the rooms were empty, save for a jumble of boxes and furniture odds and ends.

The third—the room that had been hers—was furnished with just a bed and card table where a bedside table used to be. The open closet door revealed several pairs of jeans draped over hangers and a few shirts. Other than a lamp and a stack of books on the table, the room was bare and strangely poignant. Was this evidence of Tate's vagabond life? All that he owned? For a man born into wealth on one of the largest ranches in the county, it seemed… sad. Evidence of a lonely, solitary existence.

She spared a quick glance into the bathroom, and cringed at the obvious water damage and mold creeping up the walls. The old avocado shag carpet that Aunt Millie had refused to change despite Uncle Warren's firm insistence.

Sara hurried downstairs, shivering. "Tell me that the furnace works," she said through chattering teeth. "So you can turn it on."

"Not yet. The furnace repairman has the replacement parts on back order because the furnace is so old. But spring is just around the corner, right?"

"Sure doesn't feel like it today. Aren't you worried about the water pipes freezing?"

"The water was turned off during the coldest part of

the winter, but since moving in, I've kept the fireplace going if the outside temps drop below the midthirties."

"What about that wind whistling through the window frames upstairs?"

"I've ordered new windows for the second floor. The old ones were off-brand aluminum replacements and poorly insulated. Not a wise choice."

"I totally agree. Warren installed them when I was in middle school, and I remember him arguing with Millie about which brand to buy. Warren won, unfortunately— and Millie didn't talk to him for a week."

Tate flashed a quicksilver grin. "Poor Warren."

"Her motto was always 'Spend the money and do it right the first time' and he must've finally taken it to heart, because he did a stellar job on the cabin."

Tate knelt in front of the redbrick fireplace, adjusted some kindling and slender logs and built a fire. Within minutes it flickered to life and warmth started to radiate through the room.

He rose and gestured toward an oak rocking chair, then settled on a straight-backed chair that had probably belonged to Millie's dining room set. "So, what do you think? Is there hope for this old house?"

Entranced, she watched the flames caressing the logs, the sparks rising toward the chimney then falling back as spent ash. "Of course there is. The big questions would be budget, time and intention. Who's going to live here? If you rent out the house or sell it off with a few acres for a hobby farm, you probably wouldn't want to put much into it."

"I like the idea of doing it right, no matter who lives here. The place has good bones and I think it could be something really special." He braced his elbows on his thighs and leaned toward the fire, the warm amber glow casting the planes and angles of his lean, handsome face into sharp relief. "I've spent the last ten years living out of a suitcase, going to rodeos. Maybe it's because I haven't had roots anywhere, but I've always thought I would enjoy renovating houses. Or at least trying."

She must have looked a little stunned, because he laughed and winked at her. "This probably destroys my bronc rider image, but I've spent a lot of time in hotel rooms watching HGTV."

She smothered a grin, and despite her tension earlier, she felt herself relax. "Then you and my uncle Warren have a lot in common."

"You probably won't want to tell him that. But hey, I feel I'm in good company. I've never heard a word against him."

Sara shifted uneasily in the rocking chair. "I suppose I'd better be on my way. It's getting late."

"Are you sure? I could sear some prime Angus steaks if you'd like. Wouldn't take but a few minutes."

Langford prime beef had a reputation that extended far beyond the county, and her mouth watered at the thought. "That sounds wonderful. But maybe another time?"

"Tomorrow, if you'd like—since you're coming to talk about the house anyway. Just let me know."

"I'll just come straight from work so it doesn't get so late. Can I bring something? Maybe salad fixings from the store?"

"Perfect."

At the back door she hesitated and listened to the rising wind. Swirling snow now obliterated the security light, leaving just a faint glow. It was too dark to judge the total snowfall from inside, but it was definitely time to get home.

He looked over her shoulder. "Would you rather I drove you home?"

"Goodness, no. I'll be fine."

"Text me when you get home all right, okay? I imagine that lane from the highway to your cabin would be two miles of misery in deep snow, so call me in the morning if you need help getting out. I've got a snow blade for my truck."

Touched by his concern, she nodded. "Thanks. I will, but I've got four-wheel drive and I'm a Montana girl, so this is probably nothing."

Still, electrical outages were common in this kind of stormy weather, and conjured up the image of a long, uneasy night.

"Just so you know, I think I'm going to bring the black Lab home with me tonight. The smoky smell is mostly gone and it might be nice to have some company."

"Good idea." He hesitated and for a moment she saw something flicker in his eyes—as if he was remembering their shared past. Did he ever think about their moonlight kisses? Slow dancing at the high school prom? His voice roughened. "Drive safe, now."

"Definitely." Her cell phone barked—the unique alert from her after-hours clinic answering service. "I just need to catch up on my messages, and then I'll be on my way."

He lifted a hand to touch her shoulder or maybe even offer the kind of casual hug friends gave each other in farewell. But then he let his hand drop to his side and he stepped back as if having second thoughts about crossing some invisible line.

After settling the Lab in the backseat, she started her truck, checked several messages from the clinic and made several phone calls.

She glanced toward the house as she shifted the truck into Drive.

All she could see beyond the curtain of falling snow was the faint glow of the lights inside, but she knew Tate was at the window, watching her leave. *Concerned* for her. Who would've thought the day would end this way?

This was not about romance. Nothing about fluttery feelings or hopeful expectations for a relationship that would be doomed from the start. She just had to keep reminding herself of that. But maybe it could be the start of friendship. Two adults who could enjoy each other's company and never want anything more.

Yet far into the night, while she listened to the wind howl and branches scrape against the side of the cabin, a single thought kept drifting back.

If Tate had given her that farewell embrace and if it had deepened into a farewell kiss, she definitely would have kissed him back.

Chapter Nine

Sara had texted him when she got home safely last night. Then she'd texted again this morning to ask if Tate would feed her animals, and said she'd made it to work despite the snow—though it had taken twice as long as usual and she was running late.

After his morning chores he took his truck over to Sara's to clear the lane from the highway all the way up to her cabin, then came back to begin clearing his own lane and parking area.

Just being neighborly, he told himself. Nothing more than that.

Maybe he'd felt a bit more than neighborly last night when he'd nearly given Sara a farewell embrace before she headed for home, but it had meant nothing. Just an old habit from long ago, and he'd caught himself in time.

Jess turned up just as Tate finished moving snow. He drove beside Tate's truck, rolled down his window and grinned as he handed over an insulated lunch bag and a travel mug with a lid. "Grandma was concerned about you having a hot breakfast. Everything okay up here?"

"I didn't lose power and the snow wasn't all that bad. Six or seven inches—but not much drifting."

"Down at the main ranch, I couldn't even get into the horse barn this morning until I shoveled my way through a drift in front of the door." Jess reached for his own coffee mug in the console cupholder of his truck. "So how are you holding up? This isn't exactly like the glitz and action of a rodeo circuit with your buddies."

Tate laughed. "Nope. Not close."

Jess shook his head. "When I first left the rodeo circuit to come back and help Dad I thought the home ranch was boring. But this place is even *more* isolated and lonely."

Tate snickered. "You do know how to make a guy feel good about his lot in life, Jess."

"Just checking in, that's all. You can always move down to the home place. We've got those three cabins just west of the house that are really nice now. Devlin put a lot of work into them. One is Chloe's, for the weekends when she can get back from teaching, but the other two are open."

"Nah, I'm good." Tate took a long sip of his coffee and stared through the windshield. "If you'd asked me two months ago about how long I'd last in a place like this, I would have said two days. Max."

"And now?"

"There's something peaceful about being away from life on the road. All the crowds and lights and noise. I even look forward to seeing the herds of horses and Black Angus growing fat on Langford land this spring."

Jess's eyebrows rose. "Those are words I never thought you'd say. Does that mean you want to stay, instead of trying to buy that rodeo company?"

"Nope. I'll definitely be leaving. But it's good to be home and have a chance to help you out while I can. You gave up everything to come back and help Dad, so it's the least I can do."

"Do you need help with anything up here?"

"Not yet. I can't start fixing fence until the ground is thawed enough to set some new fence posts, and I'm waiting for replacement windows to arrive for the second floor of the house."

Jess glanced beyond Tate's truck to the house. "I'm still not convinced it's worth saving. Have you figured out your reno plan?"

"Partly, but I've asked Sara to stop by and look things over. She stayed here with her aunt and uncle quite a bit so I figure she might have some good ideas."

Jess's eyebrows rose again. "The pretty little vet. So how are you two getting along? Is she going to rope you in and make you want to stay in Pine Bend for good?"

Beneath the teasing tone Tate heard a hopeful note, and he firmly shook his head to dispel any misapprehension Jess might have. "We're just old acquaintances at best."

Jess settled his coffee mug back in his cup holder. "Well, little brother, all I can say is that if you don't wake up to what's in front of you, you might be missing out on the best thing in your life. She seems like a really nice gal, she has a warm heart and she's made a good career for herself instead of living off her parents' money. Tell me you haven't thought about her over the years."

"Did anyone ever mention that you were nosy?"

Jess laughed. "So you *have*."

"Actually, no."

"Just keep in mind that your much wiser brother Dev didn't miss out on his perfect match, and he'll be getting married the end of May." Jess shot a wicked sideways glance at him. "If you hurry, you'll have time to make it a double wedding."

A dozen years back their banter would have triggered a wrestling match that lasted until they were both exhausted and laughing. Now, Tate just lifted his coffee mug in a wry salute. "Dream on. I'll be thinking of you both while I enjoy being 'footloose and fancy-free.'"

Sara finished examining the elderly basset hound—her last appointment of the day—and lifted him from the exam table to the floor. "He's looking fine, Mrs. Groveland. He had excellent lab work and a good annual checkup."

The elderly woman's diamond-encrusted rings and crimson fingernails flashed under the bright fluorescent lights when she took the leash. "I don't know what I would do without my Elmer. What family I have left is only interested in my money, but he's with me night and day."

"Well, he's fortunate to have such a wonderful owner."

"I expect he will outlive me, and I know no one will ever love him as much as I do." Her lower lip trembled.

"Do you have a relative or friend who could take him? You could leave instructions. Maybe put them in your will."

The woman's sharp laugh held no humor. "I know that if I left money for his care, my nephews would find a way to drop him off at the nearest shelter and squander every penny on themselves. They are thoughtless, selfish people and won't be getting another dime from me. I know what happens to old dogs in those shelters."

"There are no-kill shelters in some of the bigger cities in Montana. Though, if you don't mind me saying so, you seem to be in excellent health. I'm guessing you will far outlive your sweet dog."

"Then you'd be wrong, according to my doctors." The woman lifted her chin with an air of defiance. "I want to know if you can make sure my sweet Elmer has a wonderful life after I'm gone."

Sara blinked, recalling all of the times she'd been asked the same question about other dogs. Cats. Ferrets. There'd been a few snakes and potbellied pigs and hedgehogs in the mix.

"He's a lovely dog, Mrs. Groveland. I can promise to try to find him a good and loving home. But if you're talking about me taking him right now, at this minute, my home is at the breaking point and there's little space here at the clinic."

"I guess I didn't make myself clear." She waved a hand impatiently. "My family owned a pharmaceutical company for generations. My nephews are, I'm sure, looking forward to their inheritance the day I die. I plan to surprise them when I do."

Sara guessed it was going to be a monumental surprise, to say the least. One that involved finding real jobs if they didn't have them already.

"I've earmarked most of my assets for cancer research, because cancer will take me before too long. But I found some lovely, scenic property not far from here. I want to establish a foundation to run a sanctuary for old, disabled and abandoned animals."

"What a wonderful idea," Sara exclaimed.

"I need a veterinary consultant during the planning of the facilities and then on retainer for regular care of the animals themselves. I've had a bit of research done on you, Dr. Branson. You were highly regarded during your three years at a major animal emergency clinic in Chicago. And I very much appreciate the rescue work you do on your own. Are you interested?"

Sara thought of all the animals she'd taken home for refuge or rehab, the ones that were difficult to rehome. There were too many for just one person to save. If this sanctuary truly came to be, it would be a great blessing.

"I…I'd like to hear more," Sara said cautiously.

"Good." The woman headed for the door, then turned

back. "I want to leave this life knowing Elmer is still loved and that I've done something good. And I believe The Elmer Groveland Animal Sanctuary will be the answer to my dreams."

Chapter Ten

Her mind still buzzing after the surprising encounter with Eleanor Groveland, Sara hummed as she finished tossing the romaine, sliced carrots and cherry tomatoes she'd picked up at the grocery store after work, then mixed the ingredients for a homemade ranch dressing.

"It seems so strange to be here, cooking in Millie's kitchen again," she murmured as she watched Tate pour a little oil in a cast-iron skillet on the stove. "It's been a long time."

Gleaming new appliances had been delivered just this afternoon, which gave the old kitchen a look of promise, though there was much more to be done.

Tate turned the heat on high, waited until the pan was sizzling, then dropped two marinated rib eyes into the pan. After three or four minutes he flipped them, revealed a nice dark sear, poured melted butter over the top and seared the other side, then turned the temp to low. "Medium rare okay?"

"Perfect."

He sprinkled flaky sea salt on top of each one, then moved the steaks to a couple of stoneware plates and pulled two baked potatoes out of the oven. "Butter and sour cream are on the table if you want them. That's sweet tea in the pitcher."

After one bite she closed her eyes to savor the juicy, perfect steak and the pop of flavor from the crunchy bits of salt. "This is fantastic. Have you always liked to cook?"

"I do, but there aren't many chances when you're on the road all year. Steak, salmon and thick pork chops are the extent of my skills."

She took another bite and grinned. "I don't think anyone would complain if you did steaks like this every single day. I feel like I'm at a super-expensive restaurant. So what's it like, traveling all the time? Do you have a house or apartment somewhere?"

"No. But once I start working as a rodeo contractor that will need to change. I'll need a ranch for the bucking stock. I'll need to have plenty of space, so I can rotate the bulls and broncs that go out on the rodeo circuits."

"I hadn't thought of that."

"Yeah. Folks might think it's a hard life for the livestock. But good feed and veterinary care for eight seconds of work every couple months isn't too bad. Those animals are an investment, so they get treated right."

"Do you miss that life?"

"It's all I've known since graduating from college, really. It's where my good friends are. I like the adrenaline rush as a contestant. The cheers, the bright lights, and those few seconds of competition that can make or break a guy's year-end championship standings." His voice roughened and his expression grew somber. "But it's dangerous, and any one of those seconds could mean an ambulance. Or could be your last."

He fell silent.

"Were you ever hurt badly?"

A corner of his mouth kicked up in a brief, self-deprecating smile. "A time or two."

He didn't elaborate and she respected that, but when he pushed away his unfinished steak, she sensed that he was troubled about something far deeper than just a few broken bones. "A friend?" she guessed.

He ran a fingertip along the surface of his tea glass, lost in his thoughts and memories. Then he finally nodded. "The best. Jace was a devout Christian, yet all the prayers in the world didn't save him. I was with him when he died."

She hesitated, then reached across the table to lay her hand on his. "I'm so sorry."

"He left behind two little boys and a wife he loved to pieces. The irony is that he was going to quit rodeo the next month. He just about had the down payment for a nice little place in Texas where they wanted to raise their kids."

A long silence stretched between them. She wished she knew what to say that wasn't trite or condescending. Finally, she gave his hand a gentle squeeze and withdrew her own. "What a sad and terrible loss."

Tate tipped his head in silent acknowledgment. "He was a believer. He would talk to anyone about his faith in Jesus and how important it was to him. So I understand that he has eternal life in heaven and that we'll see him again someday. I just wish he was still here. His family needed him."

"And his friends."

"That too."

Tate stood and began gathering the plates, so she joined him and helped clean up the kitchen.

"Coffee?"

When she nodded, he brewed a pot of coffee and set a plastic-wrap-covered plate of chocolate-chip cookies on the table. "Grandma Betty made these. She sends a lot of food my way because she must think I'm starving on my own."

Sara poured coffee for them both, then settled back at the table. Hoping to lighten his mood, she smiled. "I hope you don't mind me asking, but are 'buckle bunny' groupies still a thing on the rodeo circuit?"

"Far as I know." He rolled his eyes. "Tight clothes, Western boots, a lot of makeup."

"Have any of them stolen your heart?" she teased.

"No. Maybe they're hoping for love, but it seems like they're advertising one thing and longing for something else."

"Do you think they ever find it?"

"That I wouldn't know." He reached for his spiral notebook and pulled out a pen. "So, what did you think after walking through the house last night?"

She took a long sip of her coffee. "There's so much potential here. In all the years Warren and Millie lived here they kept up the basic maintenance but never made any substantial improvements. You are limited only by your vision and your checkbook."

He uncapped the pen. "So if it were up to you, where would you start?"

"Obviously, the structural elements, but I'm sure you know that. The old roof leaks. The wiring and plumbing are probably outdated. But before you do anything, you'd want to imagine the overall design. Like, how you could update and expand the bathroom upstairs. And you'd also want to decide on any new dormers or even an addition on the back, before you invest in a new roof."

"The bedroom next to the bathroom is huge, but the bath is the size of a postage stamp. I can see expanding it into the oversize bedroom next to it."

She nodded in approval. "Exactly. With a walk-in

shower, in addition to that claw-foot tub. A long granite countertop with double sinks. New lighting. And a new, heated floor with a toe-kick switch that also triggers when you walk through the door."

"Sounds like a fancy hotel."

"It wouldn't need to be expensive, necessarily. Especially if you do it yourself."

"And the main floor?"

"Millie always said she wanted to put in a main-floor powder room under the stairs. She also dreamed of building an addition off the back of the house for a family room, plus a master with an en suite bathroom and a walk-in closet. She figured it would be easier for them to age in place when they got older, so they wouldn't need to move."

"Makes sense."

Sara reached for the notebook and started sketching. "The living room is a good size. But if you opened up the kitchen and dining room by taking out a wall, you could also make that space flow into the new family room."

"I suppose the lovely linoleum will need to go."

She laughed. "If I were you, I would make that a definite yes."

They sat at the table, sipping coffee and talking about the house, until the pot of coffee was empty, the cookies were gone and they finally drifted into a companionable silence.

"This has been a really nice evening," she said at last. "But I need to tell you something that I should have said long ago. I still feel bad about what happened in high school. I was horrible to you, and I'm sorry."

He gave her a wry grin. "We never did quite get it together."

"But it was my fault, and I never apologized. At the end—when you said you really cared about me, I panicked and ran. With parents like mine, just the thought of commitment at any level scared me to death. It still does."

"I can't say my parental example was any better. But you and I were both really young, so it was all for the best."

"I suppose we just avoided greater heartbreak later, but I'm still sorry." She stood and pulled on her jacket. "We talked about spending a couple evenings discussing your renovation. I usually don't work all day on Saturdays, and tomorrow I should be done at four. Will that work?"

"Perfectly. I'd like your thoughts on some of the specifics. The sooner I get my plans nailed down, the sooner I can get to work."

She paused at the door. "You know, as a little girl I used to dream about happily-ever-afters. But my dad was a cheat, my last boyfriend ran off with my best friend and the one before him walked out without a word. I'm a failure, and I am *done* with that kind of relationship. I'm so thankful that you and I can just be friends."

But on the long drive home in the darkness, she felt a small, aching place in her heart and a faint whisper through her thoughts. *Don't you want more? Isn't love possible...if you dare?*

No. There was no point. Tate would leave town in a few months. Simple friendship was safe. And imagining a glorious romance was foolish. She'd already seen where *those* fantasies ended up. Besides, her aunt and uncle would be deeply wounded if she took up with a Langford, and she didn't want to hurt them after they'd suffered enough loss already.

And this was a much safer choice.

Just friends.

It was ironic, really, coming face-to-face with someone who believed the same theory he did. Friendship was good. But beyond that, a mask of casual indifference and a "life's a party—don't take anything seriously" attitude had always been the safest bet.

In theory, it was a great plan. Exactly what he wanted.

Traveling the rodeo circuits made relationships a liability. Almost impossible. And he had no intention of starting any commitments that could tie him down to the state he'd always wanted to escape.

Added to that, the thought of being responsible for someone flat terrified him.

Yet watching Sara walking toward the house the next evening with a grocery sack in her arms made Tate imagine—just for a second—that she was coming home. To *him*. And that she did so every evening, to share a companionable meal and conversation late into the night…or perhaps a trail ride under the star-strewn sky.

He caught himself up short. That was all romantic hogwash, and that train of thought was probably Jess's fault, for ever bringing it up.

Sara knocked once and let herself inside. "I'm here," she called out. "And dinner's on me. I hope you like salmon, asparagus topped with parmesan and baby red potatoes."

Hooking his tape measure onto his tool belt, he met her at the door and carried her groceries inside. "Sounds great."

"Do you prefer the salmon broiled with herbed butter sauce or poached with dill sauce?" She emptied the contents of the grocery sack onto the kitchen counter. "Though I suppose I should first ask if you have any pots and pans."

"Grandma Betty had Jess bring boxes of kitchen supplies up here, first day I moved in. Pots, pans, spices—

she claimed she had duplicates of everything and was glad to see it go."

Sara pulled her long blond hair into a high ponytail, did some sort of magical twisty motion with her hands and suddenly it was all up in a knot on her head held by what looked like a chopstick.

He studied it for a moment, waiting for the whole contraption to fall down as she bustled around the kitchen checking the cabinets.

She pulled a broiler pan from a bottom cupboard, then found a big pot and filled it with salted water before putting it on a burner. "I figure we can eat in a half hour. Can you peel just a strip around the center of these potatoes? Leave most of the red part."

While he took care of the potatoes, she started a salad. "So, tell me about your day. Any revelations about the house?"

He finished a potato and dropped it in the pot of water. "It won't be hard to open up the kitchen and the dining room, because I discovered that's not a load-bearing wall. I figure I'll start on it after I do chores and ride colts tomorrow."

"Good news!" She tipped her head toward a corner by the refrigerator. "You'll be losing some cabinet space, but that would be a perfect place for a double set of pantry cupboards with slide-out shelves. I was looking online today, and saw some that were each seventy-two inches tall by thirty-six wide by thirty deep. You could order two of them at the lumberyard or build the new cabinets yourself."

"Good idea." He studied the corner and realized she was right. "I've been looking at the windows in the living room and dining room, and I want to preserve them. The wood frames are solid, and the multipane glass with the intricate leaded glass at the top is beautiful." He dropped the last potato into the boiling water. "Some of the windows need to be reglazed, though, as do the storm windows."

"What about the floors?"

He leaned against the counter on one hip and watched her drizzle lemon butter over the salmon, then sprinkle herbs and seasonings on top, charmed by the way she concentrated on the task.

"I've checked under the carpet in every room, and there's hardwood flooring throughout—except for the bathroom, where there's water-damaged plywood."

She shuddered. "I'm not surprised after seeing that hideous avocado shag carpeting is still in there after all these years."

"It's a wonder the fixtures haven't come right through the floor."

She waited until the potatoes were nearly done, then slid the salmon under the broiler, and added a pan of asparagus sprinkled with parmesan on the rack beneath it. Then she drained the potatoes, and smashed them with butter, salt, pepper, garlic and parsley.

"Almost ready to eat," she announced. "So what can I help you with tonight?"

The rich, buttery, herbal aroma of the broiled salmon wafted through the kitchen as she pulled out the pan and set it on a trivet, then retrieved the asparagus a few minutes later. His mind went blank as he breathed in every nuance of the food she'd prepared.

She grinned up at him, her hands on her hips. "Grab some plates, and let's eat. Then I'll help you pull up and roll carpets since that's easiest with an extra set of hands. I bought some disposable face masks in town, because I can only imagine the mold and dust underneath."

He tried and failed to stifle a grin.

"What's wrong?" She lifted a hand to touch her cheek. "Do I have something on my face?"

"I was just thinking that I couldn't have ever been so wrong about someone if I'd tried."

Her gaze narrowed on his. "You've got a complaint?"

He couldn't help himself this time. Laughing, he slid an arm around her waist for a quick hug, then he released her and went after the plates. "It's just that in high school I'd always figured you were an entitled rich girl, who'd always had only the finest and expected nothing less. Even while we dated for a while I was always a little intimidated."

"I can't imagine why." She frowned, though there was a twinkle in her eye. "And now what—you think I'm some kind of hillbilly?"

"No, I think you're amazing."

"Because I offered to help rip out that awful carpet?"

"Because—" *Because of too many things to count, and they just keep adding up.* "You just are."

She groaned and rolled her eyes. "Let's eat."

He didn't blame her. He'd never said anything that lame to a woman in his life. But he was starting to see trouble ahead, and he wasn't sure how to fix it.

She was delighted about being just friends, while every time they were together he saw more about her that charmed him. Surprised him. Intrigued him, and made him want to get to know her even better.

Which was so ironic.

On the rodeo circuit he was always the one fending off advances by the pretty young things. But he never took any of them seriously. Never made commitments. And he made sure he never, ever fell in love. In his younger days it had only led to awkward situations and unfortunate marital expectations that he wasn't prepared to meet.

But if he wasn't careful, this time it would be *him* who

was falling too hard for someone—which made no sense at all. Because he already knew there'd be no happy endings with a woman who only wanted to be friends.

And for the first time in his life, he might be the one who wanted more.

Chapter Eleven

At midnight Sara kneeled on the last roll of upstairs carpeting to keep it tight as Tate secured both ends with twine.

In this final bedroom, as with the other two, the thin carpet padding underneath had disintegrated into chunks and crumbles of foam and dust that could only be shoveled into black trash bags. The bloodied scratches on her hands and knees bore testament to the wicked-sharp tack strips rimming the perimeter of each room.

But beneath it all lay the promise of nearly pristine oak hardwood flooring marred only by the occasional water stain.

She helped him carry all three carpet rolls down the stairs to the entryway and out to the covered porch, then she ripped off her face mask, dusted her hands and placed them at the small of her back. She drew in a long breath, savoring the cold bite of the wind and the clean, pine-scented air.

"I'm not sure when I have ever felt so utterly filthy." She looked down and swept a hand over her T-shirt. "I'll bet there were buckets of dust mites in that carpet."

Tate cocked his head and studied her, then reached

out to brush something from her cheek. "And more than a few cobwebs."

He looked as dusty and dirty as she felt, but he still could've stopped traffic with that grin. She found herself grinning right back. "You've been staying here how long?"

He shrugged a shoulder. "About four weeks."

"I shudder to think of you breathing that air upstairs. If you had asthma you'd probably be dead."

"Cheery thought."

"Do you have a Shop-Vac in the barn? We can go back upstairs and clean up those floors, then mop." She stepped inside the kitchen and reached for her jacket. "You won't believe how much better you feel after—"

He laughed as he gently caught her arm to stop her. "Whoa. Not tonight."

She twisted away. "But it won't take long—"

This time he rested his hands on her shoulders to steady her. "Thanks for everything you've done, Sara. But it's late and you must be exhausted. By the time you get home it'll be one o'clock."

For just a moment she imagined sagging against his broad chest to savor his warmth. The thud of his heartbeat against her own. She wanted to feel his muscled arms around her, just as she had so many years ago—

Alarm bells clanged in her head and she stepped back, feeling a warm flush rocket up into her cheekbones. "You're right. Of course you are. Did I ever mention that I'm totally Type A about completing tasks? I'll just—"

"No worries. I'll finish up tomorrow after church," he said gently as he walked her out to her truck. "It won't take long at all. And I'll feed your animals in the morning in case you want to sleep late. Just promise you'll text me when you get home, so I know you made it. If you don't, I'll come looking."

When had anyone been concerned about where she was or if she made it safely home? It was surely only because she was so tired, but she felt her eyes burn. "Thanks," she whispered.

She drove away without looking back. But she had no doubt that he was watching her leave, and that he would be waiting for her text.

And it filled her with an unfamiliar sense of peace. Or was it something more?

Tate stepped back to let Grandma Betty slide into the pew next to Jess and Devlin, then settled in beside her. Abby wasn't back from California yet, and Chloe hadn't returned this weekend. He leaned close to Betty's ear. "Just like old times with your three rowdy little boys?"

She patted his knee fondly and smiled. "Not so little anymore, but I'm still hoping you'll all behave."

He scanned the sanctuary, looking for familiar faces.

There were a few—some local ranchers and their families. The owner of the grocery store, and several of his old teachers. But disappointment seeped through him when he realized that the faces he was really searching for— Sara, and the uncle and aunt she would probably sit with, weren't here. Maybe the snow and cold had kept the elderly couple home. And maybe Sara had slept in. She'd certainly looked exhausted when she left for home.

He settled back in the pew and looked at the tall stained glass windows that lined each side of the sanctuary toward the front. Twelve in all, they each depicted a familiar Bible story, while above the altar, Jesus with a flock of sheep filled a huge rectangular stained glass window and sent beams of jewel-toned sunshine over the pews.

The familiar scents of burning candles and lemon furniture polish brought back memories one after another.

The cloying scent of carnations and roses at Heather's funeral, her tiny casket at the front of the church and Mom quietly weeping with her arm holding him close. Mom's own funeral less than a year later, though there'd been no comforting hugs then.

Dad had been insistent about the boys showing a strong, brave face because men—especially Langford men—didn't cry. Jess and Devlin had remained stoically silent, their faces awash with tears. But at six years old Tate had collapsed with grief and someone had taken him outside until he could collect himself and return.

And then there were the less painful memories…because after that day Dad never again crossed the threshold of the church until his own funeral, so it was Betty who took the boys every Sunday.

As a kid he'd spent much of his time in church fidgeting in the pew and counting the tiny, intricate pieces of stained glass, or imagining himself in those Biblical settings. Now, from an adult perspective, he felt a sense of awe at the artistry and craftsmanship that could draw a person in with vivid colors and deeply emotional appeal.

The organist began to play "Beautiful Savior" just as she had at the beginning of every service he could remember. The congregation rose to sing the verses, then Pastor Bob led them in prayer.

When everyone sat down for the sermon, Tate caught a glint of something at the corner of his eye. He looked over his shoulder.

It was Sara, her hair loose and wavy this time, and a beam of sunshine had turned her blond hair to molten gold. A blush bringing roses to her cheeks, she slipped into the far end of the back pew.

He nodded to her and she waggled her fingertips in return.

Pastor Bob's familiar, deep voice boomed from the front of the church, and Tate settled back in his pew.

The pastor's hair had turned to silver and he was more portly than Tate remembered, but the man had called him by name and given him a jovial welcome for coming back to church.

Now the pastor's voice rolled over the congregation like a gentle wave. "Today's sermon is based on the twenty-first chapter of Matthew, verse 22. 'And all things, whatsoever ye shall ask in prayer, believing, ye shall receive.'"

"The power of prayer is so amazing, so awe-inspiring, yet some of us fail to understand and believe in this wonderful gift God grants us—the ability to speak to Him in prayer, with the understanding that He listens to each and every one of us. From the little child kneeling by her bed, to the elderly man as he lies dying.

"And He *answers*. He *always* answers. Maybe it's right away. Maybe it's in God's perfect timing that differs from ours. And maybe, in His infinite wisdom, that answer is not what we hoped. Now, what can we pray for? What should we ask? Is anything too great or too small? Let's look at Corinthians…"

The pastor's voice faded away as Tate's thoughts drifted. He shifted uncomfortably. *Prayer.*

Just the word dredged up memories of tragedy and loss, and desperate pleas that surely hadn't been answered if a loved one died anyway.

He and his brothers had prayed so hard at Mom's bedside. He and his buddies had prayed over Jace.

Though the worst had been his desperate prayers over Heather's lifeless body when she lay in the barnyard, because that had been his fault.

Betty nudged him and he realized that everyone was standing now, singing a modern praise song he didn't know. She pointed to the front of the sanctuary where the lyrics were scrolling down a large white screen.

He stared at the screen, not really seeing the words, still caught up in his old memories. After Pastor Bob led the congregation in more prayers, the service was over.

Guilt slid through him at his lack of attention as he followed the family to the vestibule, where Pastor Bob was shaking hands and wishing everyone well.

"So good to have you back, son." He gave Tate a double-handed clasp and a big smile. "It's been a long while. I hear you've been a rodeo star all these years."

His effusive praise sent heat crawling up the back of Tate's neck. "I got by, is all."

"Well, your grandma tells it differently, and she showed me a stack of championship trophy buckles you sent home to her. She's very proud of you, you know."

"Yes, I am." Betty slipped her arm through the crook of Tate's elbow and gave it a little squeeze. "But if you'll excuse me, I see someone I need to talk to."

Bob gave him a piercing look that seemed to peer straight into Tate's soul. "I'm sorry to hear you'll be leaving town again. But if you ever want to stop by and chat about anything, my coffeepot is always on and the door is always open."

"Uh…sure. Thanks."

"I always mention that to new folks and anyone who's been gone awhile, just so they know." The pastor lowered his voice. "I've known you since you were a little tyke, and couldn't help but notice that you don't quite seem like your old happy-go-lucky self. If there's anything I can do…"

"Guess I've just gotten older." Tate dredged up a smile. "Thanks, though. See you next Sunday."

He caught up with Dev and Jess at the edge of the parking lot, and Betty joined them a moment later. "You said there was someone you wanted to see?"

"Well." Betty gave a disgruntled snort. "There certainly was. That pretty little veterinarian—but I don't know what happened to her. I looked away and she disappeared."

"Ah, yes," Devlin drawled, with a wicked gleam in his eyes. "The veterinarian. Jess tells me that you two are a perfect match. How's that going?"

Jess laughed. "Yeah, Tate. If you aren't careful, you're gonna lose out to some rancher a whole lot more handsome than you are."

"Boys," Betty hissed. "Behave yourselves."

"Unlike you 'boys,' I have no plans to settle down. My life is on the road and that is never going to change." Tate jingled the keys in his pocket. "I'm going to head out. See you around."

He caught the gleam of bright golden hair just a few feet away, in the midst of a family chattering about their newborn foal. She seemed to be trying to back away and to make her escape, and when he passed she looked up to give him a knowing grin. She'd obviously overheard.

He rolled his eyes. "Family."

She said something reassuring to the people surrounding her, then she caught up with him and slipped her hand into his. "You're my getaway excuse," she whispered with a soft laugh. "Otherwise I might have been there for an hour."

"I needed an escape route myself."

Her laughter made him smile.

"Sorry—I couldn't help but overhear. Your brothers are quite the comedians. They're trying to marry you off, I take it. *To me?*"

"Sorry about that. They were just joking. Next week it'll be about something else."

"You've made it pretty clear that you want to get back on the road and leave this town behind."

"Yeah. I guess that's why they think they're hilarious. But..."

"But what?"

"When I got here I just wanted to pitch in at the ranch and help out for a while, but this town was the last place I wanted to be. I couldn't wait to pack my bags."

"And now?"

"I'm actually enjoying my time here. It's nice, smelling the pines and looking out at the Rockies at sunset every day. Peaceful. I'm glad to have this time with my grandma, because you just never know what the future will bring. And," he added with a low laugh, "despite their obnoxious manners, it's been good connecting with my brothers again."

He stopped at the far edge of the church parking lot. "I'm parked out there, but I don't see your truck. How did you get here?"

"I stopped to pick up Warren and Millie for church, but Warren didn't feel up to it." She hiked her thumb toward a little red sedan. "They asked me to take their car and fill it up."

"Well...thanks for helping me last night. I expected discussion, not hard labor. Maybe I can return the favor?"

She waved a hand dismissively. "No need. It was fun, being in that house again and imagining what can be done to it. I hope you'll let me see your progress. Millie and Warren would be so—"

She cleared her throat. "Well, I'm sure you'll do a wonderful job."

"I suppose they wouldn't want anything changed, after all the years they lived there."

"Actually, Millie always dreamed of updating everything, but there just wasn't the extra money. It's just that it was…"

"Hard to lose their home?"

She nodded.

"And a Langford making changes to their home would be painful."

"I'm afraid so. They seem to consider all Langfords as birds of the same feather, which is completely unfair. Your father handled his business, not you boys." Her voice held a note of relief, as if she were glad to unburden herself of this truth. He could understand.

"My brothers and I disagreed with him most of the time. But when you're young you don't have much choice."

"I totally understand. But my aunt and uncle are getting older now and not thinking as clearly as they once did. At this point they couldn't have stayed on the ranch at any rate—even the cabin got to be too much for them. Now I'm trying to convince them to move into one of the senior townhomes where they would have assistance."

"That's exactly where we would have been with my dad if he'd lived another decade—too stubborn to admit he needed help."

"I probably shouldn't have shared quite so much with you." She smiled faintly. "But I just wanted you to know in case you bump into them in town. My uncle has become more vocal with age, and I can't guarantee he'll be polite."

He was touched by her warning. She trusted him to understand. "I'll try not to get in his way."

She glanced at her watch. "I suppose I'd better be off. A few more hours of work on my cabin and I hope I'll be able to relieve you of your unexpected guests."

And then he'd rarely see her. It was a sobering thought.

"I've become rather accustomed to that parrot's constant singing. He's certainly a change from the radio. And the cats have apparently made themselves right at home, so they aren't any trouble. They show up for dinner and then disappear up into the hayloft."

She raised an eyebrow. "You aren't saying that you want to *keep* some of them. Right?"

"Not to adopt—when I leave Lucy will be my only travel buddy. But I know you don't have a lot of space in your cabin," he said slowly. "And that the population sort of comes and goes."

"Correct. The director of a no-kill shelter in the next county thinks they'll have room for three of the six dogs and one cat just two weeks from now. No luck on the singing parrot, though. I can't imagine why."

"So as long as I'm at the ranch, just let them stay."

"Really?" Her eyes lit up. "You are amazing."

She started toward her uncle's red sedan, then turned and gave him a quick hug. "Thank you!"

She caught him off-balance and he had to take a step back. Her hair smelled of fresh lemons and she felt so soft and sweet that it was all he could do to stop himself from drawing her into a longer embrace. *Lemons.* Who knew they could smell so good?

"Since I don't need to finish the cabin right now, I'll take the car back to Warren and pick up my truck. I need to come over to clean the parrot's cage and take the dogs out for a run anyway, so then I'll help you rip up the downstairs carpet if you'd like. Seems only fair if I can be useful." She spun on her heel and waved as she headed for her car. "See you soon!"

He stared after her, a little dazed.

One minute, he'd expected his life would return to normal...just one monochrome, gray day after another once Sara and her menagerie moved on.

But the next, he'd somehow managed to say the right thing and suddenly everything changed. At least for a while.

It was all unfamiliar ground, and he didn't even know what he should be hoping for when there could be no future in it.

But at least Sara was staying.

Chapter Twelve

Sara looked out the window at the heap of old carpeting stacked on the covered porch. "What in the world can you do with all of that?"

"I did some calling. The county landfill will take the old carpeting." Tate took a sip of coffee. "And all of those trash sacks filled with carpet pad too."

She dropped her gaze to the newly bare hardwood floor under her feet. "I didn't think it was possible, but I believe the first floor carpeting was as bad as the second. Just look at all of the stains. Generations of spills at the dining room table, I suppose. I remember knocking over a few glasses of milk myself as a kid. Are you going to refinish these floors yourself, or hire it done?"

"After watching some YouTube videos and comparing the costs, I'll do it myself. I can rent the equipment, but I'll start upstairs in the small bedroom and work my way down. By the time I get to the living and dining rooms I hope I'll be good at it."

"So you'll need all of those tack strips taken up first. I can help with those, but after that I should probably go. Is the toolbox still upstairs?"

"Yes, but you don't need to," he protested.

"I know. But then you'll be able to move along quicker and you don't have a lot of time. I can't wait to see what it looks like when you're done."

She started up the stairs, and behind her, she heard a defeated sigh.

"After all of this hard work, I really do owe you a favor," he muttered as he followed her. "What about helping you with that incinerated garage? I know it won't be replaced soon, but Jess has a front loader. We could clear it all away for you if you had a thirty- or forty-yard Dumpster dropped off."

It did look terrible—like a twisted, charred cadaver with a gaping maw where the garage door had been. Whenever she arrived home after dark and her headlights swept past it, it actually looked a little scary—thanks to watching a few too many horror movies with friends during her college days. She could almost imagine bears—or something worse—barreling out at her from the darkness.

But her mail and package deliveries went to the clinic, so no one else ever had to look at the ruins but her. It could wait.

"I know it all needs to go—every last piece of it," she said firmly. "This summer I'll hire someone to clear it all away. But you have enough on your plate already, and you're letting the rescue animals stay here. That's a huge blessing to me as it is."

Sara had referred to herself as *Type A*, and if that meant being a hard worker who didn't ever slow down, she fit the definition to a T...though why she was so all-fired insistent about helping him out he couldn't guess.

During the past two weeks she'd finished working at the clinic every day, then picked up a pizza on her way out to the ranch—or he threw something on the grill—

and they had supper together before getting to work on the house.

He'd begun to look forward to evenings all day, and their discussions about everything under the sun—politics, the latest news, global warming. Wild animal protections in the Rockies.

Spending time with a well-educated, well-spoken woman was quite a change from the chatter of the giddy buckle bunnies who dogged his footsteps at the rodeos, wanting autographs and selfies, and begging for dates. Most of them were barely twenty, some barely out of high school, and all of them spelled trouble, as far as he was concerned.

But Sara…she challenged him. Delighted him. And she'd insisted she only wanted a casual friendship, which lifted all the complications of awkward beginnings and divergent expectations. Without agendas on either side, they could both just enjoy whatever time they had and not think about anything else.

Better yet, her delight at the gradual changes in the house made him want to work all the harder. At this rate he'd reach the goals he'd set for his stay in Montana with time to spare.

He hoped she would be just as delighted when she saw her cabin after her weekend in Butte, where she'd taken a cat and three of the dogs and was volunteering two days of veterinary services to the rescue group.

Abby and Betty bustled around Tate's kitchen, putting away the leftovers of the food they'd brought over for Sunday lunch while avoiding the litter of puppies scrambling around on the kitchen floor with the twins.

"You certainly seem distracted, Tate." Jess lifted a fork-ful of Betty's blueberry pie. "Must be awfully quiet with Sara out of town. Have you heard from her?"

"I wouldn't expect to. But she did mention that she would be getting home late tonight, so she probably won't even see the garage demo until tomorrow."

"I sure hope it was the right thing to do," Betty fretted. "Just going ahead like that. What if Sara didn't *want* that all cleared away?"

Devlin laughed. "You didn't see it, Grandma. The garage was completely destroyed. We made sure we saved anything that could be salvaged but there was very little, and the rest went into a Dumpster. Tate talked to Warren Branson first, anyhow. The property still belongs to him."

Betty's mouth dropped open. "And how did *that* go? Millie and Warren have barely spoken to me in years."

"He didn't want to talk to me, either." Tate put down his coffee cup. "He hung up his phone when I called. So Jess and I went over yesterday morning and knocked on the door. We just explained we wanted to help Sara and make it a surprise, and I showed him some photos of the garage on my cell phone. I told him I would email him some photos of the job after it was done too. Once he understood it wouldn't cost him anything, he was okay with the idea."

"We even got a mumbled *thanks* before he abruptly shut the door," Jess added. "Not that we expected it. I think those folks will hold a grudge against the Langford family until the day they die."

"Well, I'll be," Betty marveled as she joined them at the table with her coffee and slice of pie. "I've always felt bad about them losing their ranch. I don't judge them for their feelings, but bitterness can eat away at a person and the only one it harms is himself. It's a sad way to live."

The family lingered over more coffee and the guilty pleasure of another one of Betty's extraordinary pies, then Abby looked at the clock and started rounding up the puppies and the twins.

"We've got school tomorrow, girls—and evening barn chores in an hour. We've got to go. Help Uncle Tate put the puppies back in their pen, okay?"

Sophie cuddled the white-and-gold puppy to her chest. "Can we keep this one? She's my favorite."

"And these two are mine," Bella announced. She sat cross-legged on the floor, with two puppies on her lap. "They're so sweet. And they love me, Mama. See? They like to give kisses."

Abby's eyes sheened with sudden tears as she bent down to pick up the other puppies and put them behind the gate barricading their bed in the storeroom. "That's sweet, but they're too young, and they would really miss their mother."

Betty leaned toward Tate. "Did you catch that? Jess and Abby have had the girls for over two years, and they've just started calling her Mama this past week. It means the world to her."

"And Jess?"

"He's still Uncle Jess, as far as they're concerned—and I'm just Grandma Betty, even if it's not technically correct. Maybe someday they'll call Jess daddy. I hope so. Lindsay has no idea of who their father was."

He hadn't known about the twins' biological father. He'd been away for ten years on the rodeo circuit, with just random visits home. "Do you ever hear from her?"

"Sadly, no. We tried to see her last year, but once she relinquished custody so Jess and Abby could adopt the twins, she wanted nothing to do with them. Though maybe it's for the best. She's still a very troubled girl."

Tate hadn't seen Lindsay since they were kids, but he remembered hearing about his cousin's behavior all too well. She'd run with a wild crowd, and had fallen into serious trouble with drugs that exacerbated her mental health issues. She'd ended up in more rehab facilities than any-one could count. Apparently the best thing she ever did for her little girls was to let them go to a loving home.

"Okay, guys," Abby announced. "Time for jackets. Our pickup is warming up, and Uncle Devlin has already gone outside."

Tate rounded up the last pup, and helped by walking Sophie out to Jess and Abby's truck. The mysteries of the car-seat buckles and straps looked too daunting, so he stepped aside and let Abby take over.

She gave him a playful nudge as he stepped back. "I promise it's not as hard as it looks. Someday this will be you, Tate."

He laughed. "Probably not."

She looked over to where Jess was talking to Devlin and Betty, and lowered her voice. "Seriously, don't let their teasing get to you. We all really like Sara and I can see real chemistry building between you."

"We're just friends, Abby."

She tipped her head slightly in acknowledgment, a faint smile touching her lips. "These things *should* take a lot of time and only you will know—eventually—if she's the right one. I'll be praying on it, though, and you should too. Especially since you'll be leaving Montana. You don't want to look back in five years and wonder why you let her get away."

"Friends," he said on a long sigh.

But the twinkle in her eyes told him she didn't believe him. Not one bit.

He opened her truck door and shut it for her after she got in, then stepped back and watched them all drive away.

Praying on it, she'd said.

Maybe it would work for Abby and Betty and Pas-tor Bob.

But he hadn't had much luck with prayers when it truly mattered, so he was pretty sure God wouldn't be concerned about him now.

Chapter Thirteen

She'd gotten back to the cabin after midnight and gone straight to bed, too tired to do more than brush her teeth and set her alarm clock.

Her hands ached from her death grip on the steering wheel. Her lower back ached after twelve spays and eight castrations at the shelter, plus a complicated compound fracture.

With three surgeries tomorrow morning, she could only hope that ibuprofen would help.

Light snow had started falling on her way home that turned to sleet, then freezing rain, making the last twenty miles slick and treacherous. The headlights had barely cut through the precipitation, leaving the road ahead a black tunnel with no highway markings visible on the asphalt.

She'd prayed most of the way home.

A text message chimed from her cell phone on the bedside table as she drifted off. Blearily patting the table, she found the phone and peered at the screen.

I hear the roads are bad. Did you make it home OK?

Despite her aching muscles and exhaustion, she smiled to herself, feeling a sense of reassurance and warmth flow through her at Tate's concern.

She had no doubt that he would've jumped into his four-wheel truck and come after her, if she'd ended up in a ditch twenty or thirty or forty miles away on some desolate road.

Home safe ten min ago. Thanx

She slid her finger over the screen to tap a simple smiley face, but with the awkward angle and darkness her fingertip slid downward and landed on a garish emoji of a dancing clown waving a banner that read SMILES!

And of course it sent, a millisecond before she could catch it.

Groaning, she flopped back on her pillow, her forearm draped over her eyes. He probably thought she was a complete idiot…and as the minutes ticked by without a response, she had no doubt.

Sleep eluded her as she lay there, still feeling the vibration of the highway in her death grip on the steering wheel, still hearing the lash of the wind and sleet against the windows and the *thump-thump-thump-thump* of the windshield wipers on high.

Her memories rolled back through the years, to the rhythm of those blades.

In high school Tate had maintained a persona of being one of the wild, irresponsible boys. Parties. Fast cars. A magnet for the fast-and-flirty girls. An irreverent class clown. A boy who got in trouble and laughed it off.

At least, that was the perception he'd fostered.

Looking back, she could remember his air of bravado, yet he'd been nothing but kind to her when they'd dated those few months. Thoughtful. And he'd been so perceptive.

He'd once found her distraught and crying, after her

dad exploded over her B+ on an exam instead of an A, and Tate had comforted her, teased her a little, until he'd actually made her laugh.

Despite her plan to shake up her parents by dating the wildest boy she knew, she'd fallen into the heady, over-whelming, emotional roller coaster of a teenager's first love.

But she'd felt guilty and ashamed too.

And when she finally told him the truth—how she'd tried to use him to gain her parents' attention, he'd walked away. It was exactly what she deserved. But it had also broken her heart.

His teenage rebel act had been only a mask, she real-ized…like the one she'd worn in the face of her parents' impossible expectations. But what she saw in Tate now was exactly what she'd glimpsed all those years ago.

He was a good man, who could take in a menagerie of rescue animals—even a raucous parrot that blared show tunes from morning till night—without a word of com-plaint. He was a better, kinder man than anyone she'd ever met. And if she weren't careful, she might start falling in love with him all over again.

Or maybe she just hadn't stopped.

Tate eased Blondie into a lope around the arena. Dropped her into a one-hundred-eighty-degree rollback, and brought her out of it and into the opposite direction on the correct lead. *Smooth as silk.*

Some days, the uncertainty of his future gnawed at him—the possibility that someone else was out there, qui-etly waiting. Ready and able to bid far beyond what he could afford, and then his dream of taking over the rodeo company would disappear like a puff of smoke.

There was nothing he could do about it. He just needed

to bide his time, and hope that the outcome was right—whatever that was.

But other days…

He reached forward and stroked Blondie's neck. Other days, it was just plain fun being back to training horses after a decade of riding broncs and racing from one rodeo venue to the next.

This was a totally different approach to riding—gentle, slow progress—but it was what he'd done for his dad as a boy, and it offered a different kind of satisfaction than hearing the eight-second buzzer. And with all that—

A text chimed into his phone. His pulse skipped a beat when he saw who it was from.

Sara: I seem to be missing a garage. Should I call the sheriff?

Tate: You were missing a garage the day it caught on fire.

Sara: Guess I owe someone a lot of money…but would dinner do for starters? Or some stall cleaning?

He laughed aloud, startling Blondie into a crowhop and nearly dropping his phone before he calmed her down.

Tate: It was a team effort. Jess and Dev helped, as well.

Sara: Then I owe you all dinner or a LOT of stall cleaning. Let's figure out a time later.

He smiled to himself as he pocketed his phone and eased Blondie into figure eights at a jog, then a lope.

During his years as a championship bronc rider there had always been flocks of buckle bunnies following the rodeo circuit—fan girls eager to catch the competitors' eyes, though he'd never been interested in one-night stands, and he'd traveled too much to ever find anything more meaningful.

But seeing Sara again was a whole new dynamic.

Come the first weekend in May, his life could change in an instant with the drop of an auctioneer's gavel…though now he was no longer sure just what he wanted that future to hold.

Pine Bend was where Sara had grown up and it was where she intended to stay, and with every day he was here, he was realizing just how much he cared for her.

Was there a chance with her if he stayed? The only thing *certain* was that there'd be no chance at all if he left town and followed his dreams.

He slowed Blondie to walk and guided her into a three-hundred-sixty-degree spin, then turned her toward the center of the arena, Abby's advice still running through his thoughts.

You don't want to look back in five years and wonder why you let her get away.

Feeling a sense of satisfaction, Tate unsaddled his fifth ride of the day and put the young mare back into her stall. It had been a good day so far. Each of the training horses was showing steady progress, and by the time he finished riding the rest of them around six o'clock he'd be ready for a hot shower, quick supper and a couple hours in front of the fireplace with his latest Tom Clancy novel.

Funny, how easily he'd settled into the routine here.

He'd spent most of his adult life driving from one rodeo venue to the next—sometimes straight through the night to make the next town in time. Staying in an endless succession of hotel rooms that all looked the same. Eating truck-stop food that all tasted the same too. A fierce sense of

competition had fueled his adrenaline and kept him moving, moving, moving. He'd never imagined that he could
find equal satisfaction in life back on a ranch.

He chuckled to himself as he led a buckskin gelding
from a stall and cross-tied him. *Yet here I am.*

Sara's dogs began yipping and barking in the box stalls
at the front of the barn. The tack room door opened and Sara
appeared. "Hey, Tate. Can I do anything to help you—"

A cat screeched and darted through the door ahead of
her. She fell in a heap onto the concrete aisle. *"Oooof!"*

"Are you okay?" Tate jogged over and knelt at her side
as she woozily braced her hands on the floor and levered
her shoulders off the cement. "Maybe you'd better just
sit for a minute."

"Can't believe I did this." She touched a scrape on the
side of her cheek and darted an embarrassed glance at him
as she gathered her legs under herself and sat up. "Aunt
Millie always told me to do the 'barn cat shuffle' if barn
cats started winding around my ankles. I didn't see that
one in time."

"They've gotten me a time or two—especially if there
are several." She appeared alert and oriented and didn't
seem to be bleeding, thank goodness. "Does it hurt to
move?"

"No…the only thing hurt is my pride."

"Did you bump your head?" Tate brushed a swath of
silky golden hair away from her face and gently lifted her
chin with a fingertip to check her eyes for equal dilation.
But then their eyes locked and he couldn't look away. *Such
beautiful blue eyes, framed with those long, dark lashes…*

She dropped her gaze, a rosy blush blooming on her
ivory cheekbones. "Really—I'm fine. Just clumsy and a
perennial victim of cats everywhere. I think one of them
sent out a memo years ago."

He helped her to her feet and steadied her with his hands on her shoulders, but his thoughts faded away as he looked down at her, entranced.

They'd spent months together in high school, but had he ever really noticed the faint dusting of freckles over her nose? The elegant arch of her eyebrows? Had he ever truly appreciated her wry, self-deprecating sense of humor?

A mesmerizing, expectant silence shimmered between them when she lifted her gaze to his, and he found himself lowering his mouth to hers for a long, sweet kiss that sent a wave of warmth straight to his chest.

From somewhere in the distance he heard Theodore screech and launch into a rap song at the top of his lungs. Tate drew back. "I—I'm sorry. I guess I shouldn't have done that."

She looked up at him with an expression of shock, her eyes wide and luminous. And then she smiled. "Just like old times, right?" she said lightly. "No worries."

No worries, maybe. But though he knew he'd just overstepped an unspoken boundary, he wanted to pull her back into his arms anyway. And never let her go.

Chapter Fourteen

Sara stood back, her hands on her hips, and studied the newly opened space between the kitchen and dining room of the old house.

Over the past few weeks she and Tate had grown closer, and she now counted the minutes until she finished at the clinic each day because they were often together. Trail rides. Hikes up into the foothills with their cameras and telephoto lenses. Stolen kisses under a blanket of stars.

And then there were the projects at either her cabin or Tate's place. But his reno project was more exciting by far. "I've been so eager to see this," she said. "What do you think?"

He draped an arm around her shoulders. "I think I owe you yet again. I was wavering about taking out that wall but this is so much brighter, and the view of the mountains from the kitchen is stunning. What do you think about an island?"

"It's your money, but my vote is a definite yes. Can you imagine meal prep there while being able to enjoy the view in every direction? You could make the far side a breakfast bar for extra seating—and an island would be a great place to set out a buffet line at holidays."

"That's what I've been thinking, but it's good to hear it from someone else who knows more than I do." He gave her shoulders an extra little squeeze, and brushed a light kiss against her cheek. "Do you think your aunt and uncle would want to see the renovations when everything is done?"

After the Langfords' generous favor in razing the garage several weeks ago—at no cost—she'd thought Warren and Millie would soften, but the most she'd gotten out of them was just a gruff admission that it was good to have the job done.

"Hmmmm…maybe."

"Some year?"

"Millie would, but I'm not sure about Warren. Losing the place was devastating for him."

"I'm sorry about my dad's part in all of that."

"Well—it was nothing that you did, that's for sure. Now Warren is starting to repeat himself—the same stories in the space of an afternoon—and he misplaces his hearing aids all the time. One day he went for a walk and he wasn't sure how to get back. Millie kept trying to tell him and he just argued with her."

The white cat Sara had given them a month ago had become Warren's shadow, and its constant presence on his lap had mellowed him some. But the visiting nurse had warned Sara that his newly diagnosed early dementia would gradually increase, and he could become more impatient and surly.

"Yesterday Millie and I went to fill out forms to get them on a waiting list for the assisted-living facility, instead of the townhomes. She went through with it, but I haven't seen her that sad in a long time."

"This reminds me to be more grateful for Betty. I think she's still sharper than any of us grandkids."

"You're absolutely right. She's amazing."

"Are you still coming over to Jess and Abby's for dinner tomorrow?"

The Langfords had started inviting Sara over for Sunday dinner every weekend, and she'd had a chance to gradually get to know them all. There were always at least nine at the dining room table, and the friendly banter never ceased to charm her. She'd only ever imagined a home like that one, and she loved every moment.

"It's like being part of a Norman Rockwell painting, and I wouldn't miss it. It was so different for me growing up." She leaned into his embrace, savoring the sense of connection. "My parents were rarely home at the same time—probably on purpose—so I often just ate alone. I only saw families like yours on TV."

"I'm getting the idea that I'm your ticket to dinners with the family you always wanted," he teased. "But I can tell you that it wasn't always so sociable. When my dad was alive he despised idle conversation and used dinnertime to tell us what we were going to be working on next. Heather could always go around him, though. She was a pretty little girl. Smart as could be and always smiling. With her, Dad was like a benevolent grandfather. The rest of us were just employees."

A shadow always seemed to fall over him whenever he said his little sister's name. "I remember hearing that she died in an accident. I'm so sorry about your loss."

"Some memories just never go away." Tate sighed heavily. "She was only four when she died—two years younger than me. Every year I imagine what she would be like on her birthday and what she might have accomplished."

"Oh, Tate. That must be so hard."

"The day she died was the worst day of my life. I was

the last one to see her alive, and if I'd just stopped her from running out of the house she wouldn't have died. It was all my fault."

Her heart aching for him, she considered his words. "But you were only six. Were you *babysitting* her at that age?"

"No, but—"

"Had someone told you to watch her?"

"No. But it should have been common sense—as I was told often enough later. And it was true. I should have been responsible. My brothers were outside somewhere and they should have been watching out for her too."

"Blaming you boys was terribly unfair to all of you." Sara considered her words carefully. "What…happened to her?"

"Dad was angry about something, and he was leaving for town in a hurry. He didn't see her, and he backed right over her."

"So he didn't watch out for her, either. As the driver, he should have checked first—anyone with kids and dogs should know that. It was his fault. Not yours."

"In his big dually with oversize tires, he couldn't have."

"Again—it was his responsibility. He was the *driver*. He should have looked."

At the turbulent expression on Tate's face, she guessed she'd maybe gone too far, and when he headed for the back door she didn't follow.

Her heart heavy over what the Langford boys had gone through and the guilt Tate still carried, she quietly gathered her jacket and purse and let herself out the front door.

Tate went out to the barn to do chores early, then switched his boots for running shoes and headed up the trail leading to the highest point on the Branson ranch.

The snow was gone now, the quiet little creeks of summer gushing with the heavy spring runoff coming from up in the mountains.

On the sunny side of the house he could see plants beginning to poke tentative tips of greenery through the soil, but up here everything was still winter brown and desolate.

It served his mood perfectly.

No one ever understood what had happened when Heather died. It was easy to lay blame if they hadn't been there to see Dad's blind fury. To hear him roar to the heavens about his stupid, stupid sons.

Dad had always responded to lacerations and broken bones with angry outbursts—quick to accuse the injured child of being careless, and angry about the inconvenience. It made no sense, even after Betty tried to explain that it was the loss of control that made him feel helpless and angry.

But the day of Heather's death had been horrible on so many levels that to Tate it was a long and painful blur. It had spurred Dad's anger even more, when Tate stood in front of him, mute and miserable, and unable to explain how he'd failed to protect his sister.

But Jess and Dev were older and made of stronger stuff. They had borne the greatest onslaught, and for them the blame went on and on despite Mom's and Grandma Betty's pleas.

Forgiveness had never been part of Dad's lexicon. And until the day he died, he blamed everyone but himself for the death of his little girl.

Chapter Fifteen

The church smelled of lilies as Sara walked into it on Easter morning and hesitated at the back. The pews were nearly full already. She could see the Langfords in their usual place halfway up on the left, with Abby next to Jess and the twins, then Devlin and Chloe. Betty sat at one end of the family group and Tate at the other.

She'd sat with the family last Sunday and everyone had smiled and scootched a bit closer to make room, but after yesterday's awkward scene with Tate over Heather's death, she wasn't sure of her welcome.

He'd been the one to walk out of the house first and she'd wanted to give him space to relive his ongoing grief. She also suspected he'd wanted to escape *her*. He hadn't called or texted since.

So be it.

For weeks they'd been together most every day, and each day they'd seemed to draw closer. They cooked together, worked on projects together. Laughed and talked and teased each other over silly things, and it had seemed as if they'd been friends forever…and maybe more.

Obviously, she'd been wrong.

Slipping behind a group of men talking cattle prices,

she went to the back pew on the far side and sat behind a tall woman with an even taller hat bedecked in lilacs. It was an awful hat but excellent camouflage, so she could avoid attracting any attention from across the church and just concentrate on absorbing the Easter message—her favorite of the entire church year.

The organist was just beginning the first notes of "Beautiful Savior" when she felt a bump at her side and someone crowded into her.

She didn't even need to look to know it was Tate.

"Why are you way over here?" he whispered.

She gave him a sideways glance as the congregation stood up to sing. "I assumed you were still upset so I'm giving you space. I'm just not sure if it's supposed to be temporary or permanent."

She picked up a hymnal from the rack on the pew in front of her and found the right page, but as she started to sing he reached up to support half the hymnal and began to sing, as well.

His deep, rich baritone seemed to slide over her like warm molasses, and she found herself listening to the sound of his voice instead. *Who knew he had a voice like that?*

After the pastor led the congregation in prayer, everyone sat down for the sermon. Tate casually reached over and entwined his fingers in hers.

Pastor Bob looked over the congregation, his face filled with joy. "Today, on this most glorious day of the year, we celebrate our risen Lord. We begin with John 11, Verses 25 to 26. 'Jesus said unto her, I am the resurrection, and the life: he that believeth in me, though he were dead, yet shall he live: And whosoever liveth and believeth in me shall never die.'"

Sara settled back in the pew, absorbing the wonderful

message. Thankful that she'd come today, to celebrate Easter with this congregation of believers—many of them people she had known all her life. Thankful too that Tate had come over to sit with her, evidence that all was well despite their brief rough patch last night.

After the service Tate threaded her arm through the crook of his elbow and they walked outside into the sunshine together as a couple.

When they were away from the people gathered outside the church he bent his head closer to hers. "I'm sorry about yesterday. This week is always tough for me but usually I'm on the rodeo circuit somewhere. With people who don't know anything about what happened."

"So you never have to talk about it."

"That's about right."

"And how does that work out for you?"

He thought for a long minute. "It's just a lot easier."

That sure sounds healthy. But she bit her tongue instead of saying it aloud. It was his right to manage his grief in his own way, and this had been his choice for years.

"Happy Easter, you two." Jess strolled over with Abby and the twins at his side. He glanced at Tate's and Sara's entwined arms, then looked up with a knowing smile. "Are you two coming out for Easter dinner?"

Betty caught up with Jess and frowned. "I certainly hope so. Chloe and Dev have already left so they could check on the ham, and I've planned plenty for everyone. Even Abby's dad and stepmom, though it turns out they're driving to Butte this afternoon so they can fly to Vegas in the morning."

Abby chuckled affectionately. "You'll understand when you meet her, but Darla dearly loves the flash and glitter of Las Vegas, so Dad takes her there every year. They

don't drink or gamble—she just loves all the lights, stage
shows and fancy buffets."

"She wears twinkly dresses," Sophie announced. "Pink
and purple."

"Glitter and jewels too," Bella added with obvious awe.
"Except not real ones."

Sara smiled down at them. "You girls look pretty spar-
kly yourselves. Exactly like princesses."

"Let's go, everyone." Jess took Betty's arm and herded
the girls toward his Expedition. "It's time for Easter dinner and I don't want to be late."

Betty and Abby's Sunday and holiday dinners were always incredible, but Easter was Tate's favorite, bar none.

Smoky bone-in ham. Tender Langford prime rib.
Poached salmon and dill sauce. A colorful array of a dozen
different side dishes and salads, plus fluffy homemade
rolls that practically melted in his mouth.

By the time dinner was over and the dishes done, he
was pretty sure he wouldn't need to eat for a week.

But then, after the girls had found the Easter baskets
hidden in the yard, there was Betty's towering lemon
meringue pie, and her browned-butter pound cake, to be
topped with sliced fresh strawberries and the homemade
vanilla ice cream that had been churning away during
the meal.

Betty eyed him affectionately from across the table.
"I do so love a young man with a good appetite. Especially when he never seems to gain an ounce no matter
how much he eats."

Devlin coughed and slid a dry look at Tate. "I'm sure
there was a compliment in there somewhere, Tater. Just
keep looking."

"I was just thinking about how many Easter meals I've

missed with y'all. Way too many. It's good to be home this year."

Betty's gaze took in everyone at the table, then landed on Tate. "There's nothing I love more than the times when we're all here together. Nothing is more special than that. Have you thought about giving up those rodeos and just being a rancher?"

He felt an expectant silence drop over the room like a curtain, as if everyone held their breath.

"I've thought about it. But I've been looking for a solid, successful rodeo company for years, and an opportunity like this is rare. If I don't bid, I'll always wonder if I could have done it."

Dev lifted an eyebrow. "So what's it gonna be like, watching all of the other cowboys compete for glory while you're in the back lot babysitting the bucking stock?"

"Sure—I'll miss it. But I'm considered an old man at thirty-two, compared to those younger bull and bronc riders, and with a decade of injuries behind me it's getting harder to compete." He realized he was rubbing the knee that had sent him to a surgeon twice, and reached for his coffee instead. "I'd rather quit when I'm still halfway good, than be a has-been racking up a lot of failures."

He looked over at Sara and raised a brow. She nodded, and they both gathered their coffee cups and dessert plates. "I suppose I'd better be heading back home to do chores."

Betty scurried over to the refrigerator and withdrew two grocery bags that she handed to Sara and Tate. "I'm sending leftovers home with everyone. You too, Sara. We'll never eat it all here."

Sara smiled and gave her a quick hug, then turned to Abby and Chloe. "Thanks so much, everyone. This was the best Easter dinner I've ever had."

Abby grinned. "Next year, we'll ask you to do the mashed potatoes. Hopefully there'll finally be one person in the family who doesn't end up with lumps."

Chapter Sixteen

Next year...

Easter had been an entire week ago, and Abby's words about next year were still ringing in Sara's ears.

Is that what everyone in Tate's family was expecting? That she and Tate were a couple heading toward rings and wedding bells?

If so, they'd forgotten to send Tate the memo, though they could be pardoned for their mistake.

He'd held her hand during the Easter service, and *that* bit of news—PDA between the new lady vet in town and a Langford—had probably been observed and spread through the town like wildfire, because not that much happened in a community the size of Pine Bend.

And then he'd compounded it when he'd firmly looped her arm through his as they left the church—like a newly married couple heading down the aisle after their I Do's.

Why had he done that?

They'd resolved to be just friends, and she'd try to stay that course, even if she sometimes found herself dreaming about what it would be like to look forward to a lifetime with the one man she'd loved—and lost—so many years ago.

True, she'd been here at his ranch every day since Easter, taking care of her animals and helping Tate and Devlin with the house reno. It filled her with joy to help bring Millie and Warren's old house to life. But he hadn't followed up on that public display of affection with anything more and she hadn't had the courage to bring up the subject.

Sensing that the end of a relationship was coming was one thing. Being told was another.

He probably hadn't meant anything by holding her hand or taking her arm in his. Maybe he'd had second thoughts. But at least she could be with him for his last three weeks in Montana before he left to chase his dreams.

Shaking her head, she knelt in the layer of warm black soil she'd bought to spread along the foundation of Millie and Warren's old house. Pulled a few weeds, then carefully sprinkled fertilizer around the perennials Millie had nurtured through all the years Sara was growing up.

The days were cool up here and the growing season short, but Millie's wildflower gardens had once bloomed in a beautiful riot of color, and Sara intended to bring them back to their former glory.

Even if it was a waste of time.

With Tate still planning on going to the rodeo auction the first weekend in May, the flowers would barely have a good start before the house was empty again.

And whoever moved in, whether buying or renting, might not even care about them.

Still, this was for Millie, not anyone else. If Sara could coax the early spring flowers to bloom, she would bring her aunt up here to show her that someone still cared about her old home.

Last week, roofers had installed a new steel roof. Devlin had built a kitchen island and installed new cupboards, while Tate rebuilt the upstairs bathroom and installed a new powder room downstairs. This week Tate and his brothers had refinished the wood floors both upstairs and down, and they'd installed the new insulated windows upstairs.

The more substantive changes—like a new three-season porch—would be in the future, unless the house and a few surrounding acres were sold.

At the sound of tires crunching on the gravel drive, she stood and shaded her eyes.

Tate climbed out, grabbed a duffel bag out of the bed of the truck and strode up the walk. "Hey, stranger."

He'd been looking for ranch property in Colorado that would be far more centrally located than the Langford ranch for the base of his future rodeo company. Seeing him coming toward her after just three days apart made her pulse skip a beat and sent warmth to her cheekbones. He was the only man who'd ever had that effect on her, and she doubted anyone else would ever come close.

Despite her best intentions, it was getting harder to imagine the future without him. But soon he would be walking right out of her life and it apparently didn't bother him at all.

"Any luck finding property?" Just asking made her heart still.

"Not yet. The ranch listings closer to Denver were too pricey for what they were, and without enough acres for rodeo livestock. The properties farther out needed too much work. I'd need to bulldoze the house and barn and start over, on all of them."

If she tried to express sympathy it would just be a lie. She managed a faint smile.

He tossed the duffel up onto the porch and sat on the

top step to survey what she'd done. "So all of those little weedy things are flowers?"

Dusting the dirt from her hands, she rolled her eyes at him. "You have no idea. The entire foundation of the house and the perimeter of the yard were once an absolute showpiece—a profusion of wildflowers my aunt planted so there would always be beautiful color from late spring through early fall. It was quite a feat, up this high in the foothills. She was once featured in a local magazine. They called the place a jewel—a miniature 'Monet's Gardens of the Rockies.'"

"She really loved this place," he said slowly.

"Warren did too. It was their home for over forty years." Sara sat down next to him. "If I can nurture these flowers along, I want to bring Millie up here so she can see them again before…well, before someone else moves in."

He leaned forward to rest his forearms on his thighs and wove his fingertips together. "I—I'm no longer sure that will happen."

"What? I thought the place would be rented or sold after you left."

"That was the original plan, yes."

She watched him quietly, expectantly waiting. "What changed?"

"I had a lot of time to think during the drive back from Colorado, and I'm not sure I should let this go."

Her breath caught.

"I keep thinking about something Abby said to me. I just don't want to lose something important that I can't get back."

Their eyes met, locked. She felt a shiver of hope and anticipation race down her spine.

"I don't know if I'm even *capable* of putting down roots…or real commitment," he admitted. "You know what Dad was like. My parents' marriage was a disaster from day one. I think my mom was even more miserable that last year of her life because of him…and me."

"What?" Startled, she searched his face, wondering if he'd misspoken. "After losing Heather she must have treasured you boys beyond measure. How could a sweet little boy of six ever make his mother miserable?"

He stared off toward the mountains. "I managed pretty well."

"I don't believe it."

"I was wild. Disobedient. I acted out all the time. My grieving mother had to deal with a perpetually wild kid who drove her crazy."

"She said that?" Sara asked carefully. "Really?"

"She didn't have to. Dad made it very clear."

Sara felt her heart wrench for the little boy he'd once been, grieving his sister's loss as much as anyone but too young to be able to express that tumult of emotions. His parents might have been too wrapped up in their own sorrow to see it. She reached out to rest a comforting hand on his arm. "I'm so sorry."

"Be sorry for my mom. When she died of a heart attack, Dad figured the stress I caused played a big part in that."

Aghast, Sara tightened her fingers on his arm. "That isn't true. And frankly, it was horrible of him to say it."

"It always made sense to me." He lifted a shoulder. "I've been thinking about it. Maybe that's one reason I left home and rarely came back—it was always easier to stay away than come home and face the truth and the memories."

"The *truth*? If I could stand in front of Gus Langford right now, I'd give him a piece of my mind—and then some. Why would anyone burden a child with such horrific guilt?"

Tate didn't answer.

Please, Lord—let me say the right thing. "I…I took a class on death and dying while I was in premed. I read that young kids have a hard time understanding the finality of death. If it happens, it's like an earthquake in the family—everything changes. Mom and Dad are grieving and seem like different people. There's little joy. The feeling of security is lost."

Tate nodded.

"I also read that young kids can be so desperate for everything to go back to normal that they'll subconsciously try to distract parents from their loss and grief. Act out. Cause trouble." She tilted her head. "I have absolutely no doubt that your mom understood that and loved you to pieces. Your dad was wrong."

He stared somberly at his hands. "I'd like to think that."

"No, *believe* it. Even if you *were* difficult at times, all little kids are. Have you taken a good look at Bella and Sophie and heard them whine and bicker?" Sara thought about her own parents, their marriage repeatedly torn apart by unfaithfulness. Her lonely childhood. "But I do know what you mean about commitment. Trust is hard when you haven't come from a stable home."

"Or one where everyone got along." Tate fell silent for a long time, then he cleared his throat. "I'm thinking about staying right here, and running this ranch."

"Really?"

A corner of his mouth hitched up into a wry quarter smile. "Six months ago I would have laughed at the thought, but I like being here. Ranching. The stability. Being with family…and with you."

And with you.

Those three simple words seemed to shift the earth off its axis. And yet, did he truly realize what that meant for the future he'd always dreamed of? "What if you lose your chance to buy that rodeo company and no other opportunities come up for years? Will you regret it?" She held her breath, praying for the right answer.

"What I'd regret is not choosing to stay right here." He rested his hand on hers. "So now that we have that settled, Dr. Branson—it's Saturday night. Can I take you out to dinner?"

After their talk on the porch they went to a little steak house in the next town and talked until midnight over coffee and candlelight.

Then the next day they went to church and the usual Sunday dinner at Jess and Abby's place. Probably a mistake, because everyone except the twins seemed to sense a change in their relationship, and Jess and Dev began making premature assumptions about the future.

At some point during the chatter over the dinner table Abby announced that she, Jess and Betty were going out of town Monday to handle a routine doctor's appointment for Betty, and Tate found himself offering to do Jess's chores and watch the twins overnight. What had he gotten himself into?

He found out when the little live wires got off the school bus at three o'clock on Monday afternoon.

They raced to the barn and climbed high into the hayloft searching for new kittens—which made him imagine falls from high places, broken bones and emergency room visits.

They wanted to ride their elderly pony.

Play with their dog, Poofy.

And they begged at least fifty times for a drive over to

his place to see the puppies and the irritable parrot, though the prospect of turning them loose in a house still filled with sharp tools and electric saws and building materials filled him with dread. At that, he gave them an emphatic *no*.

Once he herded them into the house they wanted one snack after another and then managed to turn the place upside down with toys and dolls and art projects. By the time Sara showed up at five thirty, he was ready to collapse in a chair.

"So," she said, hiding a smile as she surveyed the damage. "It looks like you've all had a *very* good time. Was it fun playing with your uncle Tate?"

"I wish Momma was here," Sophie said with a bleak expression. "I miss her."

"Me too," Bella added glumly.

"Well, here's the score, ladies. I'm going to make supper while you two put everything away. The toys, the art projects and the dolls scattered everywhere."

Bella stuck out her lower lip. "But we're still playing. And Sophie made the most mess. Not me."

"Did not!"

"Both of you, get to work. After supper, your mom's directions say you'll have some homework, bath time and books, and then you go to bed."

"But—"

"Everyone will be home before your bus arrives tomorrow afternoon, so we can't have the house all messy for them, right?"

An hour later Tate loaded the last of the supper dishes into the dishwasher, then turned to watch Sara calmly helping the twins with their homework at the kitchen table. Who knew that first graders had homework these days?

Or that it took an entirely different skill set to corral

two rambunctious little girls? He had a feeling that they'd instantly sized him up as a pushover, and that he needed to learn the power of simply saying *no*.

Now, sitting quietly at the table with Sara, they were perfect little sweethearts.

All three had long blond hair that gleamed beneath the rustic chandelier hanging over the table, and he felt his heart catch at the way the girls had pushed their chairs right next to hers. If Sara ever had kids, he imagined they might look just like the twins with their gleaming molten-gold hair. The thought made his heart warm.

Kids. Family. When had he ever given that sort of life a second thought? Yet now...

Sara looked up at him and gave him a curious look. "You're staring. Is something wrong?"

"Nothing at all. Thanks for coming over to help out," he said with a heartfelt sigh. "What did you think, girls? Did you like Sara's macaroni and cheese?"

Bella looked up from the worksheet in front of her. "It was yummy. The biscuits too. But I wish Momma and Daddy were home."

"And Gramma Betty," Sophie chimed in. "They promised to come home tomorrow. But maybe they'll miss us and come sooner."

Sara shook her head. "They had to take Betty to an early doctor's appointment in Bozeman, sweetie. But one of them will be at your bus stop when you get home from school tomorrow."

Bella industriously labored over her worksheet for a few minutes and then looked up. "You're staying with us overnight, right?"

"I'll tuck you into bed, but then I'll go back to my cabin. Tate will be here, though. He'll be in one of the guest rooms just down the hall."

Sophie's eyebrows knit together with worry. "But we want *you* to stay. Uncle Tate doesn't know how to make ponytails or help us get ready for school. And he prob'ly doesn't know how to make breakfast, either."

"Or about the school bus," Bella added.

"It's a little disheartening, hearing that I've been judged a flop in the temporary-dad department by a couple of seven-year-olds," he said dryly. "I haven't even *tried* making a ponytail. Maybe I'll be a prodigy."

Sara chuckled. "Abby left three pages of detailed notes, so everything is covered, girls. I'm sure Tate can manage ponytails, and before bedtime I'll help you pick your outfits for tomorrow, okay?"

Tate glanced at the wall clock. "While you three are busy, I'd better go out and check on a mare. Jess figures she'll be foaling sometime in the next twenty-four hours."

"Which means you could end up in the barn for a long while sometime tonight," Sara said slowly. "Do you need me to stay so there's someone in the house for the girls?"

"Yes!" Bella cried at once. "You can have a sleepover with us. We could make a blanket tent and everything."

Tate was pretty sure that would mean a lot of giggling and no sleep. "Let's think about that," he said as he pulled on his jacket and boots. "And we'll talk when I get back from the barn."

There'd been nothing in the forecast. But during the last couple hours the wind had come up, bringing sleet that encased everything in a thick layer of ice and made the barnyard treacherous. Out in the barn, he found the mare in active labor and foaling perfectly well on her own, but by the time he got back to the house an hour later the precipitation had changed over to a heavy curtain of snow.

No one would be going anywhere, for a very long time.

* * *

"I miss Momma," Bella said, her eyes filled with tears. "And Daddy too. What if they don't come home? What if they got *frozen*?"

It was so sweet to hear the girls finally referring to Jess and Abby as Mom and Dad, but their deepening attachment also made the separation harder. "We know they're safe, right? They're still at a hotel in Bozeman, nice and warm. When the highways open they'll come home right away."

Sara wrapped both twins in a hug in front of the wall of windows in the great room. The world outside was nothing but an expanse of white, but inside the fireplace crackled merrily and at least there hadn't been a power outage. With plenty of food in the pantry plus the chest freezer downstairs, they'd be fine for however long the snow lasted.

Tate had used Jess's snowmobile to get back and forth to do his own chores, take care of Sara's animals and move Lucy and her puppies out to a warm box stall in his barn. With over two feet of new snow on top of heavy ice, and drifting that made everything even more impassable, the main highways were still closed. In Montana, one just never knew. Even in late spring.

"It's been forever," Sophie whispered. "Is everyone at school but us?"

"All of the schools are closed. And it hasn't been forever. We've been snowbound for just two days. You've had fun, right?" Sara surveyed the network of blanket-covered chairs creating tents and tunnels throughout the living room. "You two have the best forts ever. And did you ever guess what a good storyteller Uncle Tate is? Or that he knows some magic tricks?"

Bella's expression filled with worry. "But he's been outside a long, *long* time. What if *he* got frozen and doesn't come back?"

Sara involuntarily glanced at the time on her phone. "Well, nothing is easy with all of the snow to deal with. The chores here seem to take about two hours, then there's all of the chores over at the other place plus the long snow-mobile round trip to make it back and forth."

With chores twice a day at each place, he seemed to be working from dawn till dusk, and by the time he came in for supper she could see it in his weary expression.

Still, bless his heart, he had played with the girls and read to them each evening while Sara cleaned up the kitchen and got the girls' bathtub ready.

When she'd arrived Monday night the house had been a disaster zone and he'd clearly been out of his element with the young girls. But by the second night he'd certainly hit his stride—hearing all of the laughter and listening to him tell them tall stories with his deep, expressive voices had charmed her completely.

"I hear the snowmobile!" Sophie shouted. "He's coming!"

The girls ran to the windows and pressed their noses against the glass, eagerly watching as the bright head-lights cut a swath through the lightly falling snow, then veered toward the barns.

He would be a wonderful dad, someday, Sara thought with a little tug at her heart. Though when the date of that rodeo auction came would he really decide to stay here, or would he follow his heart?

She was pretty sure she knew.

Two weeks after the blizzard the snow was gone, the sunshine bright, and even before she got out of her truck,

Sara could see the twins were over the moon with excitement.

Abby and Chloe waved as she strolled over to greet them, then they all turned to watch Tate unload a black-and-white paint pony from the horse trailer.

"He's beautiful," Bella exclaimed. "Is he mine?"

"We'll see how each of you girls do with him, and then we'll decide," Abby said. "This one is Charlie."

Sophie gave Abby a worried look. "Is there another one?"

Abby kept a firm hand on each of the twins' shoulders to hold them back. "Let's wait and see."

Devlin and the pony disappeared through the door of the horse barn, and soon Jess backed a bay-and-white paint pony mare out of the horse trailer. He led her into the barn and cross-tied her in the aisle.

Abby smiled. "This one is Francis. I just love her name, don't you?"

"Can I pet her?" Sophie cried, fidgeting impatiently. "Please?"

To Sara's eyes the ponies looked about as excitable as manatees, but it still was important to take things slow at first. "It's up to your parents, but they might be a bit nervous right now, so they need to settle in first. This place is all new to them."

Abby nodded. "We can watch while Sara does a health exam on them, girls. You can pet them after she's done. But you won't get to ride them for a couple days."

They all trooped into the barn, then stood aside as Sara examined each pony carefully. "Excellent," she said at last. "They both appear sound and healthy. They'll need their teeth floated, but I'm due at the Parker ranch in forty-five minutes to check on a new foal, so that will have to wait.

I'll do their springtime vaccinations today, though. Do you have any tubes of paste wormer handy?"

Jess looked at his watch. "In the house, so I'll give it to them later. Dev and I need to head out in a few minutes."

Sophie and Bella looked up at Francis with awe, then edged closer and began petting her. "Do you think Lollipops will be sad 'cause we got new ponies?"

He was probably relieved that they'd outgrown him and delighted with his retirement to pasture, but Sara just smiled. "You can always pet and brush him too. He'd like that."

"We won't ever sell him, girls," Abby said. "He'll always have a home with us. And who knows—maybe he'll have a new little rider someday."

Everyone turned as one to look between Abby and Jess. That small, secretive smile and the glow in her cheeks were a dead giveaway.

"Oh, Abby—I'm so thrilled for you!" Chloe gave her a heartfelt hug, then stepped back to look at Abby head to toe. "When?"

"Late October."

Abby looked at Jess with a smile so filled with love and happiness that Sara's heart caught, then melted. "Congratulations—both of you. This is so exciting!"

It was hard to imagine feeling such joy.

She glanced at Tate and their eyes met. Held. And then he gave her that heart-stopping quarter smile that never failed to enchant her.

Especially after this past week.

They'd once resolved to be friends. But after they decided to ditch that charade and see where that led them, she'd discovered a side of him she'd never expected. The tall, broad-shouldered rodeo cowboy was a true romantic at heart. Who knew?

Their days were still filled with work, but at night he brought her flowers. Took her to dinner. And—he'd even watched three chick flicks without complaint, back-to-back. Maybe they'd once tried to maintain the distance of good friends, but he was definitely making up for it now.

They'd even started talking about a future together and Tate told her he had never been happier.

The pony lifted her head and snorted, her ears pricked. Bella turned toward the barn door. "Momma! Who is *that*?"

A slender, curvy figure posed in the doorway, one hand on the doorframe and the other on the hip of her short, short, short cutoff denims. Behind her Sara could see the rusted tailgate of an old green Chevy pickup.

In the doorway she was silhouetted by the afternoon sun, but there was no mistaking that pause for effect, or the feline grace of her walk as she headed straight for Tate.

Sara's mouth dropped open, then she clamped it shut when the woman slithered straight up to him, flung her arms around his neck like a needy octopus and planted a kiss square on his mouth.

"Uh…girls, we need to go back to the house. *Right now.* I…forgot something. Cookies. We need to make cookies." Abby grabbed the twins and hustled them out of the barn. "You too, Jess. *Now.*"

Chloe shot a sympathetic glance at Sara, turned away to grab Devlin's arm and then they too were gone, leaving Sara to watch in frozen horror as the woman leaned back a little and framed Tate's face with her scarlet-tipped fingers.

She gave him a seductive smile. "I've missed you. It's been way too long, so I thought I'd better check on you. You need to come back."

The woman's cowboy hat wasn't a Resistol or a Stetson, the Western boots were more flash than function. She wore a tight Western plaid shirt that exposed her flat, willowy midsection.

She looked like a cowgirl version of a human Barbie doll, and Tate wasn't exactly resisting.

So this was what he wanted—flash and sparkle, not some ordinary woman who usually wore plain vet-clinic coveralls with a stethoscope slung around her neck.

Embarrassed, humiliated, Sara felt her cheeks turn to flames. Then she too escaped the barn to leave the happy couple—especially the lying, deceptive cowboy— in peace.

Before she said something she would regret.

His words came back to her as she drove away and she gritted her teeth. He'd once said buckle bunny fan girls wore tight clothes, Western boots and a lot of makeup.

He hadn't said he *didn't* have any buckle bunnies in his past. He'd only said that he *discouraged* them. And he'd described the woman in his arms to a T.

It was certainly a revelation, and Sara only wished she'd seen it sooner. If this was the kind of woman he pre-ferred, then these past weeks had been a farce. Probably just something to while away his time as he waited for the auction and his rodeo life to begin again.

She had been a fool.

Chapter Seventeen

After checking on the newborn foal at the Parker ranch, Sara went home to shower and change clothes.

Going back to Tate's place to quietly pick up her remaining animals was too great a risk right now. He and his long-lost girlfriend had probably gone there to continue their reunion, and the thought of running into them again made her stomach clench.

Instead, she headed for Pine Bend to check on a post-surgery case at her clinic, and then went to check on Warren and Millie.

Millie's welcoming smile turned to worry the instant she opened the door. "Oh dear—come in. Is something wrong?"

Warren leaned forward in his recliner to peer at her, then leaned back. The white cat, like always, was in his lap. "She looks fine to me."

"I am, Uncle Warren. Maybe just a little tired."

Millie's expression of concern didn't waver. "Come, have a nice cup of tea. I made banana bread this morning. Would you like some?"

"Just tea would be fine." She could detect the aroma of Millie's moist nutmeg-and-cinnamon-spiced banana bread, but today she knew it would taste like sawdust. "Can I make the tea for you?"

Millie flapped a hand in dismissal. "Just go say howdy to Warren. He's been in a bit of a mood today."

Sara sat next to him and rested a hand on his. "Are you feeling all right?"

"Hhhhmpf."

"Is that like A-okay? Or just middling?"

"Ask your aunt. She's the one who thinks we need *assistance*. I'm fine staying right here."

"Ahhh." Sara shot a questioning look at Millie.

"He opened a letter from the assisted-living place," Millie said when she brought over two cups of tea and then went back for her own. "It could be months or even a year before they could offer us an apartment." She rested a hand on Warren's arm and raised her voice so he could hear clearly. "It won't be anytime soon—even if we wanted to. And we can always decline."

He stroked the cat with a gnarled hand. "What if they don't take cats?"

"They do, Warren. Remember? It's right on the contract. I promise you we won't ever go anywhere without your cat."

From what Sara could see, they would need assisted living sooner rather than later, and declining wouldn't be an option.

Warren's eyes grew heavy and he seemed to be dozing off. Millie tipped her head toward the kitchen table and touched a forefinger to her lips.

At the table, she cut two slices of banana bread and set out butter, plates and forks. "Now, tell me what's going on."

"Nothing, really." The understatement almost made Sara laugh.

There wouldn't be anything going on ever again, thanks to the surprise appearance of Tate's girlfriend. No walks under the stars. No late-night talks in front of the fireplace.

No talk of a future together.

"Well. I don't believe you, but I don't want to pry, either." Millie stirred sugar and a little milk into her tea. "So I'll tell you something instead—and it's something I'm ashamed to admit."

"I can't believe that. You're the kindest, sweetest person I know."

Millie snorted. "I wish that were true, but we're all sinners and I've done my share. And far more."

The fragrant scent of the banana bread proved too hard to resist. Sara gave one to Millie, and took the other. And then she waited for Millie to continue.

"I fancied I was a good Christian. I always go to church—or the chapel service they have at the Senior Center. I read my Bible and try to hold my favorite verses in my heart."

Sara nodded.

"And I *know* only God has the right to judge others, not me, no matter who or what they are. It's sinful to hold a grudge. We're supposed to love each other, not hate."

Now Sara knew where this was heading.

"Yet I've spent eight years despising a neighbor and extending that resentment to his entire, innocent family. Resenting all of them for what in truth was our own failure."

"The ranch," Sara said quietly.

Millie nodded. "I've only wanted to lay the blame on Gus Langford's greed. But in truth, we would have lost the ranch anyway, before long. Warren could no longer manage all of the work. Our medical bills were staggering. The drought…" Her voice trailed off. "Well, maybe Gus escalated things. But that's just who he was. My job was to forgive, accept what was and move on with grace. And I failed."

Sara's own debacle today suddenly seemed very small, and she felt a flash of guilt for dwelling on it. "I know it was hard on you, and I am so sorry."

"When you came back to town I warned you to stay away from the youngest Langford boy. I thought he was no better than his father, so I told you that you deserved more."

"I remember."

"Do you know he came right up to our door one day?"

Sara's mouth fell open.

"To my shame, there probably isn't a person in town who doesn't know how Warren and I felt about that family. Yet Tate and his brother came to our door, knocked, and Tate talked to us. He didn't back down when Warren raised his voice. He just waited him out, then explained again. All he wanted was permission to do you—and us—a great kindness."

Realization dawned. "He asked your *permission* to raze the garage?"

Millie nodded. "He wanted to take care of it for no cost, and he wanted it to be a surprise for you when you got home."

She'd thought he'd simply come over to do it, not realizing that he'd had the class to ask. She swallowed, thinking about the other ways Tate had been thoughtful and kind.

"He even puts up with obnoxious parrots," she said softly.

"I don't know anything about parrots." A sad smile touched Millie's lips. "But a little bird told me that you were with Tate Langford at church on Easter, and that he seemed to be sweet on you."

Seemed to be was certainly correct.

"If that's true, I don't want you to miss happiness because of anything I've said about him or his family. He's a fine young man, and I was wrong to judge. I just want to ask your forgiveness."

Feeling uncomfortable about any further awkward encounters with Tate and his girlfriend, Sara lingered at the café in town over an early supper until Tate would have completed his chores, then she slipped out to his ranch.

His truck was gone, she noticed with relief, so she collected the parrot, three dogs and the only two rescue cats she could find, left him a terse note about the missing cat, and then headed for home.

As she drove up to the cabin she surveyed the space where the garage had been—an empty twenty-two by thirty cement rectangle where Tate and his brothers had worked so hard to surprise her.

Kind hearts. Thoughtful people.

Even if one of them was completely dishonest.

She didn't expect to see them much anymore, though. The delightful Sunday dinners, celebrations for births of babies and other family events wouldn't include a veritable stranger once Tate was gone.

She let the three dogs run for a bit before bringing them inside, brought in the cats, then picked up the parrot cage and lugged it into the cabin.

She pulled off the fabric cover. "Almost dinnertime, Ted."

The miffed parrot ruffled his feathers, stretched out his wings and twisted his head to peer at her with one beady golden eye. He launched into his favorite rap song, then paused and started again. *"Emergency! Emergency! Ringadingding!"*

She laughed. "You got that right, buddy." But the cabin

no longer smelled of smoke, and life was good—except for a minor hiccup—and she'd forget him soon enough.

A text chimed into her phone.

Then another.

Any emergencies would come via her pager, so she turned the phone off and tossed it on the counter.

If she'd only heard secondhand about Tate's relationship with some floozy, she wouldn't have taken it at face value. She would have talked to him. Worked at being fair. Discovered the truth. But what she'd seen wasn't just a tale spread by a malicious gossip.

That woman knew him. Kissed him as if she'd done it a thousand times, and he certainly hadn't pushed her away.

It was time to move on, and that's what she intended to do.

Chapter Eighteen

Sara had intended to move on with her life and not look back. She had no doubt that Tate would return to his original plan, head for the rodeo company auction in one week with his scantily clad friend and start his new career.

She didn't expect to see him show up at the clinic first thing the next morning with two crates of barking puppies.

Wishing Neta was here to greet him, she slid a glance to the appointment book on the front desk. "Vaccinations," she said wearily. "Come on back. First exam room."

The puppies were all fat, wiggly bundles of pure energy, and it took a while to give each one a simple exam, administer its vaccinations and fill out a health form Tate could give to its future owner. With their wildly different colors, at least it was easy to keep track.

She put the final pup back in its cage and handed Tate the stack of documents. "They all seem to be in excellent health," she said stiffly. "Neta isn't here today, so I'll have her send you a bill."

He lifted the cages. "About yesterday—"

"No need to explain."

"But—"

"This whole situation is awkward and a little embarrassing, to tell the truth. But I understand now. We're just friends, Tate. And I'm honestly not interested in anything more. I do wish you the best, but please don't feel you need to offer any excuses." She ushered him toward the front door, then turned to the next client and waved her toward the hallway. "Second exam room on the right, Mrs. Conway."

There were several clients with dogs and cats in the waiting room and Tate's puppies began barking excitedly at all of the interesting new scents. Sara heard the noise fade as he went out the door, then stop as the door closed behind him.

She listened for a moment, almost wishing he would come back inside and tell her in no uncertain terms that he'd sent the other woman packing. That yesterday there'd been a terrible misunderstanding and he cared only for her. But Sara was no fool, and she knew that was unrealistic.

Or was it?

She'd seen a flash of raw emotion in his eyes when she'd turned him away a moment ago…just enough to make her second-guess her feelings and give her a small ember of hope.

But when Sara left for home at five o'clock, she saw the rusted tailgate of an all-too-familiar green rusty Chevy truck parked in front of a strip motel on the edge of town.

And there was Tate's truck, parked right beside it.

Tate tossed his hammer in the toolbox and stripped off his leather gloves, then stepped back to survey the work he and Devlin had done on the Branson house over the past week. "So what do you think? Pretty nice?"

"I think you should stay right here instead of gallivanting all over the country. Been there, done that, and I still don't get why you want to leave all of this behind. What kind of life is that?" Devlin pulled on his faded denim jacket. "You've got a fine place here, in a part of God's most beautiful country. You have family. Grandma, who isn't going to live forever."

He had a point, but Tate just shrugged. "I can always visit."

"Whatever." Dev pocketed his billfold and cell phone on his way to the back door. "Drive safe tomorrow, Tater. And good luck. Just remember what—and who—you could have had here if you hadn't messed it all up."

Tate couldn't argue with that.

But he'd done what he came to do—he'd helped Jess and Dev as much as he could with what time he had, and he'd already taken the training horses back to the main ranch for Jess to keep riding.

During his time back home he'd discovered a surprising truth. He truly wanted to stay. To live out his life as a rancher, and be closer to his family.

But the thought of living in Montana, knowing he would still run into Sara and maybe see her marry someone else, made it easier for him to leave.

After a sleepless night he threw his duffel bag in the back of his truck before dawn, took one last look at the house and headed south toward Denver.

It was twelve or thirteen hours, with stops for fuel and food. If the weather stayed clear and traffic light. He'd be at his hotel by evening and at the auction at noon tomorrow. And if the good Lord was willing to answer his prayers, he'd soon be the owner of a rodeo company and well on his way to the life he'd always wanted.

His headlights cut a narrow swath of light through the darkness as he drove on, then a faint pink blush began creeping above the eastern horizon. He turned the radio on, then off. Shoved a CD into the slot but tired of that too. Dev's words were still running through his mind when the sun was high overhead.

Dev had made it sound so easy. *Just go talk to her*, he'd insisted.

But Dev hadn't seen the look of disgust and hurt in her eyes when she'd ushered him out of the vet clinic and told him he shouldn't come back. And Dev hadn't tried to text her a dozen times or send emails that she'd probably deleted on sight.

Tate had tried to explain as best he could, in those messages, but Sara hadn't responded to them—perhaps she hadn't even bothered to read them. And that told him all he needed to know. She didn't trust him. And she definitely didn't care.

He'd always known he wasn't worthy of a woman like her—even before the incident at the barn. And he'd finally given up.

He drove a few more miles, and Dev's words hit him again. Why was he so driven to leave Montana and spend his life on the road?

It wasn't about the money earnings and the big gold trophy buckles anymore. It wasn't the adrenaline rush of competition and seeing his name rising in the standings for year-end championships.

Now that his days of competing were over, he could see the bare truth.

It had never been about the glory. He'd needed to leave his past behind. The tragedies and heartbreak, and the expectations he could never meet. Dad had died years ago, but was he still trying to earn acceptance and love from a man who'd had none to give?

And what about the one person who he knew was the

love of his life—was he willing to walk away from her, as well?

After Sara broke up with him in high school he'd donned the mask of nonchalant indifference he'd hidden behind after the deaths of Heather and his mother. It had been the way he'd survived that pain as a kid and he'd used it ever since. To risk loving someone was to risk facing devastating loss. It was never worth the pain.

But maybe it was time to let that go and instead take chances.

With all of his efforts at maintaining a platonic relationship, he hadn't allowed himself to truly see what was before him—a lovely, inquisitive, dedicated woman with a loving heart.

He hadn't realized how wonderful it was to see someone every day. To build on a relationship with shared experiences and deepening trust.

The conversations and laughter, and holding Sara close to kiss her good-night before she left for her cabin had become the highlights every day.

How had he been blind for so long? He'd tried to run from commitment all his life, but this time he wasn't going to make that mistake.

Glancing in his rearview mirror, he turned sharply up the exit ramp ahead, and then he headed for home.

The bells above the front door of the clinic jingled just before the noon closing time on Saturday.

Sara stopped writing some notes on the last dog she'd seen for the day and listened, hoping it wasn't another emergency.

At the familiar voice she stood, then hurried to the front desk, where Neta was writing a receipt for a payment on account.

"Hey, Jess."

He looked up at her and smiled. "Good to see you. It's been a while."

"A couple weeks."

"Just because my brother can be stupid doesn't mean we don't all want you to come out. You're welcome to Sunday dinners every weekend, if you'd like."

She nodded, knowing that she would never take him up on the kind offer. It would be awkward, being out there without Tate…rather like a pesky remora still trying to cling to a family that would never be hers. "How is Abby feeling?"

He grimaced. "Mornings are pretty miserable. I feel so sorry for her."

"I suppose Chloe and Devlin are busy with their wedding plans?"

He chuckled at that. "I wouldn't know, except for the ongoing discussion about where to have the ceremony. Dev thinks the church is easier. Chloe wants someplace outside with lots of flowers. The only thing I know for sure is that it will be Memorial Day weekend so their friends have more time to travel."

She fell silent, not wanting to ask more.

"As for Tate, this is the day of that rodeo contractor's auction," Jess added. "So he left yesterday. If it goes well I suspect we'll only see him a few times a year."

There was a thread of sympathy in Jess's voice and she knew he was probably thinking about that humiliating scene with Tate and his…friend, and feeling sorry for her. "I hope he does well."

Neta handed him his receipt and he slid it into his billfold, then she gathered up her coat and purse, waved in farewell and headed for the back door.

"We all think he should come back." Jess hesitated.

"You do know that the woman who showed up at the ranch is a buckle bunny who has dogged him for several years, right? She somehow tracks him down and then just randomly appears. I told him he needs to renew his restraining order."

Was that true, or was Jess just trying to defend his brother?

She might never know for sure. "That must be really difficult."

"Just wanted you to know." He settled his Stetson in place and walked out the door. She locked it behind him, then leaned against it, thinking.

Jess had come in to make a payment that he easily could have sent by mail or paid online, and he'd come at the end of the morning when the other clients had left. Had he really just wanted to tell her about Tate?

It was honestly kind of sweet of him, but she'd *seen* Tate's truck at the strip motel, and excuses didn't matter. The relationship was over.

Tate had turned out to be just like her unfaithful father. And that was something she could never forgive.

Chapter Nineteen

Sara's phone chimed just as she was leaving Millie and Warren's apartment on Sunday afternoon. She glanced at the screen, then did a double take.

Tate: I'm back for just a few hours and have caught your other cat. Please come and get it—there'll be no one here to feed it. House door open.

She glared at the screen. Then sighed.

She could have happily gone forever without seeing Tate Langford again.

Yet…if he let the cat loose, how would she ever catch it? It might disappear into all the little nooks and tunnels between the bales in the loft, and she could spend hours trying to find it to no avail. If there weren't enough mice around, it could starve.

She tapped out a quick OK. Be there in twenty.

Added a grumpy emoji.

Then had second thoughts and deleted it.

When she arrived at the house she felt a pang in her heart at the wispy wildflowers starting to bloom along its foundation. Soon there would be a profusion of color if someone were here to water them, but that didn't seem likely now.

Tate stepped out onto the front porch and waited for her to walk up the stairs. "Thanks for coming."

She frowned, trying not to meet his eyes. "Where's the cat? Is she in a carrier?"

"Inside."

He opened the screen door and she stepped in, prepared to see the reno projects she and Tate had worked on. But the scene was disconcerting. Unfamiliar. Was everything *pink*?

She yanked her sunglasses off and stuffed them in the pocket of her jean jacket, then blinked.

Every flat surface in the kitchen and great room was covered with rose petals.

"What is this?" She faltered. "I don't get it. Is—is this some kind of joke? Where's the cat?"

She surveyed the room again, half-afraid she was hallucinating.

"The cat is in a carrier by the door." Tate stood a few feet away from her, with a tentative quarter smile. "I didn't know how to at least have a chance to talk to you. I know you are—or were—really upset, and I don't blame you a bit."

She glared at him. "This doesn't change anything, Tate. You *lied* to me. All the while we were together, you had some other woman stowed away somewhere—someone who apparently was missing you and wanted you home. You two obviously know each other *very* well."

"Not in the sense you mean."

Sara shuddered. "Is she here?"

He shook his head. "Open the folder on the counter and take a look."

Keeping a wary eye on him, she lifted the cover with

a fingertip, then looked down at the thick stack of documents inside. "W-what is this?"

"Copies of restraining orders. Five years' worth, because each only lasted twelve months. You'll also see records of violations of those orders. I never invited her here—half the time I have no idea how she tracks me down."

So Jess hadn't been trying to cover for his brother after all. He'd been telling the truth.

"But that *kiss*."

"Her obsession, not mine. If you imagined that I was kissing her back, you didn't look close enough." He shrugged. "She has mental health issues, obviously. I don't dare shove her away and risk harming her—or get her riled, because then the situation can really go downhill. I just wish she would stay away."

"But you were at that motel." Sara narrowed her eyes at him, watching for obvious deception. Her dad had been a skillful liar too. "I saw your truck next to hers when I drove by after work."

"True, but I was in my truck, waiting for a deputy to arrive so I could identify her. Sometimes she ends up charged with harassment, sometimes they lock her up for a while or she spends time in a mental health facility and then they let her go. This time they're sending her back to her family in Colorado. I'm not her only target, by the way. I hear she's fixated on a number of other rodeo cowboys."

Sara felt like a deflating balloon as her tension and anger slowly dissipated. She brushed a hand over a scattering of rose petals. Picked a few up, then looked up at him and managed a wobbly smile as a flood of emotions rushed through her. Relief. Joy. Wonderment. And love. "I thought these petals were real!"

He ducked his head and gave her a sheepish grin. "Not

possible in Pine Bend, but I had these overnighted by Amazon, hoping the surprise might help. I was afraid you would turn on your heel and walk out."

"I…I don't know what to say."

"All I want is another chance. I want to work harder at this and try to get this right." He moved toward her and gently took her hand in his. "I was halfway to Colorado when I came to my senses and realized I was driving away from the one person I'll always love. You."

Epilogue

Abby reached out to adjust the wildflowers in Chloe's hair, then stepped back to check the effect. "What do you think—is that right?"

"You are the most beautiful bride I've ever seen," Sara murmured. "I'm so happy for you and Dev."

Chloe reached for her and gave her a big hug. "I can't thank you and Tate enough for working so hard on these flower gardens. When I saw what you'd done I just knew this was the perfect place for our wedding."

"They were my aunt Millie's pride and joy when she lived here. I brought her up a few days ago to see them and she was so touched, she burst into tears. She's thrilled to see them brought back to life."

Abby leaned a little closer and lowered her voice. "So… anything new between you two? I keep noticing how Tate watches you from afar—like he's afraid you'll disappear."

"Disappear?" Sara laughed. "Not likely. The vet clinic is booked solid for the next three weeks, and I've got meetings with Mrs. Groveland about the animal sanctuary she wants to build in Pine Bend. Plus, I've promised Tate I'd come up to tend the gardens for him through the summer.

The most exciting thing—after this wedding—is waiting for that late-October baby of yours. How are you feeling?"

Abby chuckled. "A lot better now. For which I'm *extremely* grateful."

Pastor Bob wound through the small crowd of friends and relatives to Chloe's side. "If you're all set, we can begin in a few minutes. Your violist is ready to start."

"Yes!" Her eyes sparkling, Chloe impulsively gave him a quick hug and a kiss on the cheek, then she went to find Devlin.

"That is one very happy bride," Abby said with a chuckle. "I'd better round up my not-so-ladylike flower girls before they end up with grass stains on their dresses."

Sara scanned the yard. "They were with Betty a few minutes ago and now all three of them have disappeared. Good luck."

Sara stayed at the edge of the lawn, her heart overflowing as she surveyed the gathering.

Millie and Warren had come, and were sitting on a stone bench holding hands. There were some folks from church, friends of the family and a few of Devlin's old military buddies. Chloe and Devlin had preferred a simple ceremony over Memorial Day weekend, with just people they knew well.

Tate moved to Sara's side and slid his arm around her waist. "Does Chloe know about the phone call yet?"

"I don't think so… Dev took the call yesterday and he wanted to surprise her during the wedding toasts before we eat. I can't imagine her happier than she is right now, though."

Against all odds, the family had somehow managed to keep the secret for an entire day—a phone call from a publisher wanting to buy the cookbook Chloe had so lovingly written.

After the wedding ceremony, everyone drifted inside to the kitchen, where a bountiful buffet had been set out on the kitchen island and the dining room table.

Tate brushed a kiss against Sara's cheek. "Come with me for a minute—I want to show you something."

He led her through the house and out to the front porch, then shut the door. "I've wanted to ask you this for a long time, but I never found the right moment. Maybe this is too soon, and this is the wrong time, but I just want you to know how much I love you, Sara—I never knew I could love anyone this much. And after nearly losing you I just don't want to take that chance again."

She looked at him, her knees trembling, as he pulled a small box from his jacket pocket and handed it to her. She gasped when she opened it and found a delicate gold band with a perfect solitaire diamond.

"Marry me?"

She'd never imagined this moment. Never imagined loving someone so much that an eternity together wouldn't be enough.

She stepped into his embrace for a long, long kiss that warmed her heart and filled her with joy. Then she looked up into the silver-blue eyes that had entranced her since senior high, and gave the only answer she could. "Yes— absolutely and forever, yes."

* * * * *

Dear Reader,

Thanks so much for joining me for the final book in my Rocky Mountain Ranch series for Love Inspired! I really hope you enjoyed following the last of the three Langford brothers as Tate overcame his troubled past and found happiness and love back in Montana.

If you missed the first two books in the series, they are *Montana Mistletoe* (November 2018) and *High Country Homecoming* (June 2019) and can be found at www.harlequin.com.

I love to hear from readers, and can be found at PO Box 2550, Cedar Rapids, Iowa 52406, or online at www.roxannerustand.com; www.Facebook.com/roxanne.rustand; www.Facebook.com/roxanne.rustand.author; and by email at: roxannerustandbooks@yahoo.com.

Wishing you good health, happiness and blessings in the coming year,
Roxanne